Martina Mackenzie

~*~*~*~

The Diana's Eye

Thanks Lilly!
I hope you enjoy this!
Cori Nicole Smith

CORI NICOLE SMITH

MARTINA MACKENZIE
THE DIANA'S EYE

www.facebook.com/pages/Cori-Nicole-
Smith/96602895198

Rinesmith Carothers Publishing House
Pittsburgh, PA

For information, address Rinesmith Carothers Publishing House at Rinesmith.Carothers@gmail.com.

Cover art by Liza Phoenix, LizaPhoenix.com
Printed in the United States of America

Library of Congress Cataloging-in-Publication Data

Smith, Cori Nicole.
Martina Mackenzie: The Diana's Eye / Cori Nicole Smith.
ISBN: 9781434887542
Rinesmith Carothers Publishing House

Special thanks to:
*Mom and Dad for sending me to college and
being my biggest fans
*Sandi, a great writer, editor, and friend, for her
insight on the novel
*Elizabeth, Michelle, and Martina for reviewing
and discussing
*Emily, my first critic and the castle's namesake
*And Martina, also, for being the first Martina

~*~*~*~

Table of Contents

~*~*~*~

Chapter 1 - Mr. Willoughby's Gift

The last day of school was always the longest, and Martina Mackenzie, a seventh-grader at Starry Fields Middle School, experienced that discomfort to the fullest degree. Had she known what was to happen that evening, however, the day would have been even longer from the anticipation.

Not only was she expected to gaze at her teachers under the guise of paying attention for another three hours, twelve minutes, and twenty-nine, twenty-eight seconds, but she also had to contend with a funeral that afternoon. Exhaling slowly and counting the number of ceiling tiles again, Martina ignored Mr. Almos, who was excitedly blabbering about . . . um, something historical? Probably. It was a history class after all.

Again, her thoughts turned to Mr. Willoughby. He had been like a grandfather for her. Ever since her family bought his house and ice cream shop, Willoughby's Sundae Best, he had been a frequent visitor in their home. He always told intriguing stories about everything anyone could possibly imagine, way better than anything Mr. Almos said. "Once upon a time, in the not so far away world of Sheardland . . ." Mr. Willoughby would begin. "Sheardland" always sounded so mystical and magical and just plain wonderful. Martina wished she were there right now.

Martina twitched uncomfortably as Mr. Almos droned on, and then she remembered she must sit as still as possible to keep from getting a run in her tights.

Sitting in the stiff wooden desk chairs would not have been half as bad had Martina not been forced to wear tights that morning. But, her mother insisted that "young ladies do not go bare-legged to funerals," and she was appalled at the suggestion.

Martina's dark grey dress wasn't half as fun as the pink Capri pants and matching striped top she wanted to wear. She had spent the entire day trying not to get her tights caught on the underside of the wooden desktop. Wearing uncomfortable clothing must be the best way to honor Mr. Willoughby's memory.

After the final bell rang, Martina raced from the building, shouting to her friends to make plans for their excitingly empty summer days. The sun felt good on her skin as she burst forth from the institution, but it blinded her after being inside all day.

Her mother waved her over to their SUV. "Do you have everything from your locker, hon?" she asked.

Martina nodded and tossed her bag into the backseat beside her six-year-old brother, Teagan. As she slumped against the seatback, she pulled her long auburn hair up over the headrest.

"Mooooooooom, her stuff's on my siiiiiiiiide!" Teagan whined. He furrowed his eyebrows.

Their mother, Caroline, started into a speech about how to behave at a funeral as they drove through the school zone and onto the main road toward the funeral home.

*   *   *   *   *   *

At the funeral, Martina's first, she wasn't surprised to see the mass of people who pressed in around Mr. Willoughby's casket. So many heartfelt stories were told, but none as magical as Mr. Willoughby's own.

What stuck most in Martina's mind, though, was the inscription on his gravestone: "Look deeper than the surface / Gaze beyond what can be seen / Don't accept reality as an answer / Things are not always as they seem." She knew it echoed the words of one of his favorite poets, the name of whom she couldn't remember. The words played over and over in her head, sounding otherworldly. She could almost hear Mr. Willoughby saying them. The thought was soothing.

"Jörgen Jaska!" she almost cried out when she remembered the poet's name. When she first heard it, the name made her laugh because it sounded like a character in a fantasy novel. She thought that Jörgen Jaska would fit right in, in Sheardland.

*   *   *   *   *   *

After the funeral, the family drove to their house, number 248, on the corner of Cranberry Lane and Poppyseed Place. It was a massive Victorian-style home built by Mr. Willoughby himself. Throughout the house were rich hardwood floors of a wood that no one could quite name. The long wrap-around porch housed the entrance to the ice cream shop and was covered by a roof decorated with Martina's favorite part about the house: white gingerbread trim, almost like in a fairy tale!

That evening, the ice cream shop was closed in honor of Mr. Willoughby. With no customers to attend to, Martina thought she could idle away the hours by planning her summer vacation. Instead, she and her brother were asked to clean up and restock the shop. "Working already," she thought grumpily, and she had only been out of school a few hours.

Martina hurried toward the door, eying Teagan as he examined an especially sticky booger between his index finger and thumb. As she entered the shop, her brother shoved her, with his not-so-sticky hand.

Their dad, Sylvester, was perched at the top of a ladder changing one of the light bulbs. "I'm glad to see you two getting along so well."

Martina took the hint, but she wasn't sure if Teagan got Dad's sarcasm.

Suddenly, as she stood in the ice cream shop, Martina felt almost at peace with Mr. Willoughby's death. Yes, she would miss him greatly, but he had trusted her family to run his ice cream shop. He always said that his mission was to bring a little magic to the world by squirting it into a cone. She remembered him pointing out the look of absolute happiness on a three-year-old girl, despite the sticky sweetness oozing down her chin as she devoured her ice cream. "Now that's magic!" he said. Knowing that it was up to her to continue his mission, she smiled and looked at her brother. He never quite looked magical with food on his face.

Martina gazed at the sparkling machines, thinking about how magical it would be to pump the ice cream directly into her mouth. If only she could flip each handle in turn—vanilla, chocolate, and swirl—and let the milky goodness slither down her throat. A warning look from her father told her he knew exactly what she was thinking.

"The walls in here remind me of Mr. Willoughby," Teagan said.

The iridescent constellations painted there had been his star chart.

"Remember when Mr. Willoughby told us about how the constellations got their names?" Martina said.

"Those were some good stories," Teagan answered. "I liked to hear about his adventures in Sheardland, too."

"Me, too," Martina said. She toyed with the handle on the vanilla, tightening the tip so it wouldn't fall off the next morning. Then she and her brother helped restock toppings, cones, bowls, and spoons and put everything away. Dad led them back into the house for dinner.

"It's been ten years since we bought this house and store from Mr. Willoughby," Mom commented.

She pulled her shoulder-length curls into a ponytail and sat down to dinner.

"It doesn't seem that long," Dad said.

"Why did Mr. Willoughby sell this place?" Teagan asked through his partially-chewed chicken. "He was here all the time after he sold it."

"Close your mouth when you chew," Mom said. "I've never been sure of that myself, sweetie. He told us he had top secret work he needed to do instead. He was such a character. He probably got pretty lonely here night after night without his family." Mom smiled at Martina and Teagan.

"I could never get lonely with all this ice cream," Teagan said.

"Speaking of ice cream, Ves, we're short one mix container again," Mom said to Dad.

"That's been happening off and on all year" Dad said, noticeably puzzled. "I called the manufacturer, but they said they sent the right amount. Whenever the guy takes it off the truck, though, it's usually one short."

As the family grew quiet, the newscaster on TV rambled on about the flooding in southern Asia due to a second week of extremely high tides.

"Why are the tides so high in Asia?" Martina asked.

"I read an article online earlier that said scientists are still baffled about it," Mom replied.

"I wonder if it's from climate change," Martina said. "I hope they figure it out before it gets worse."

Suddenly, the doorbell chimed. "I'll get it," Dad said. He slid out of his chair and strode toward the door.

Martina could hear soft talking from the front hall. A minute later, her father entered with Mr. Willoughby's great-granddaughter, London, who was carrying a red shiny box. Martina smiled at her classmate.

"Hey Martina, Mrs. Mackenzie, um, Martina's brother," London said. "Sorry to interrupt, but my Mom asked me to bring this." Her voice was much more hushed than normal. London still had on her stylish black dress from the service, and the dour expression on her face told them that she had not completely left the funeral behind her.

"It's no trouble at all," Mom said. She smiled kindly at London.

London held out the box hesitatingly. It was about the size of a ten-gallon fish tank and covered in red crinkly paper peppered with gold astronomical charts that glinted in the evening sunlight pouring through the dining room window. Carefully, she set the box on the table as Mom cleared a spot by the mashed potatoes and green beans.

Martina and Teagan, who until now had remained motionless in their chairs, jumped up to see the box.

London placed her hands on the top of it, though, and made no motion to open it. "Mom was putting something away in my great-grandfather's closet this morning, and she found this box with a note on top." She plunged her right hand into her jacket pocket and pulled out a folded piece of paper. She flipped the note open and placed it on top of the box as well.

London attempted to read her great-grandfather's scrawl.

"Dearest Ian,"

"The note's for my dad," London added.

"Please give this box to the Mackenzie family if I am unable to do so myself. Martina and Teagan will appreciate the gifts inside. They will find them very useful in the near future. I have taught them everything they need to know involving the project. Remind them I'm very proud that they can continue my work.

— Your loving grandfather, Artemidoros Ezra Willoughby"

London paused and wiped her eyes with the back of her hand.

Martina struggled not to cry as she watched London's reaction to her great-grandfather's words. She gave London a quick hug to make her feel better.

Remaining silent, London sniffed and folded the note to put it away.

"What work is he talking about?" Teagan asked. He received a stern look from both of his parents, probably for breaking the silence.

"I suppose the ice cream shop." London's voice still shook slightly as she looked back at the folded note.

"Hey London," Teagan said, "Mr. Willoughby told me one time he was too old to run the ice cream shop anymore. He said he couldn't keep up with the customers, but I think he wanted to eat the ice cream instead of making it. Making it is hard work!"

London smiled for the first time since she arrived. "You're right, Teagan." Sniffing again, she said, "I don't know what's in here, but I'm sure you'll like it. Great-granddad was the best at giving gifts. It's like he knew what you wanted even if you didn't know yourself."

Finally London cautiously lifted the lid. The inside was crammed with newspapers wadded up for packing material. Sifting through the box, London came up with a small cube-shaped object wrapped in more newspapers.

"Teagan," London read from the tag as she handed him the newspaper gob.

Teagan reached for it and began furiously ripping it apart. As the pages fluttered to the floor, a box was revealed. Mom grabbed Teagan's hand, slowing down his excited unwrapping. Soon though, Teagan ripped the box open and pulled out a watch that appeared to be nothing special at all. In fact, Teagan wrinkled his nose in disgust. He depressed the button on the side. To everyone's surprised, he was greeted with a loud, high-pitched, rhythmic beeping. It seemed that his gift was broken. Teagan smiled politely and thanked London.

"I'm sorry," London said. "I didn't drop it or anything. Maybe it's supposed to do that." She cocked her head to the side and smiled.

Teagan's face suddenly brightened, and Martina knew he was thinking about how he could torment her with the sound, a game that ranked a close second favorite to his first: collecting Scary Ugly Combat Monsters trading cards. He stowed the watch in his pocket.

London dug through the box again and, after pulling out nearly all the newspapers, managed to retrieve another package. This one was also wrapped in newspaper but was tagged for Martina.

Martina accepted the gift and set the heavy object on the table. She gently tore the paper from the package. Inside, she found a sweet-smelling box that was completely hand-carved from a dark wood.

Martina slowly opened the lid, which creaked a bit on its unused hinges. The inside was also carved from wood and had been intricately painted. It was a music box with a model of the Sundae Best ice cream shop with a circular track running through it.

"Wow, this is so cool!" Martina exclaimed.

She turned the box around and found a key protruding from the back, which she wound.

Rather than the tinkling noise emitted from a normal music box, this one produced a smooth, flowing sound much like a string quartet, like the one she had heard her cousin play with.

"Pretty!" Martina said, grinning.

As the song played, a tiny figure came out the door between the house and shop and crossed over to the ice cream machine. Then, the three handles on the front of the machine turned to the open position. The front of the machine flipped open, and the tiny wooden figure passed through the opening. Next, the entrance closed, and the cycle began again.

"It's Mr. Willoughby!" Martina pointed at the little man in the box.

Everyone gathered close around Martina and peered at the figure as it made the circuit again. There was no mistaking it. The tiny man had on the same sort of outfit that he usually wore, including a bow tie covered in stars, Mr. Willoughby's favorite. Even the hair matched his perfectly, with very fine cotton fibers attached in a wispy replica of his haircut and beard.

"Wow," London muttered as she stared at the music box. "I wonder where Great-Granddad got it."

"It must be handmade," Dad commented, "and by a very talented artisan."

Martina grinned. It was the most beautiful gift she had ever received. She wound the key again, tightly, and watched the little man pick up speed, dashing through the door and into the ice cream machine.

"Don't wind it too tight, hon," Mom said. "You don't know how old it is."

"I'll be careful," Martina said. She was fascinated by the tiny replica of Mr. Willoughby. From the corner of her eye, she saw Teagan trying to press the button on the watch in his pocket with the table edge to draw attention to himself.

"Well, I ought to be going now," London said as she walked toward the door. "My mom will have dinner ready soon."

"Thank you for bringing that box over," Mom said.

"Thanks London! See you later," Martina called as she let her out the front door.

London headed down the walk. She pulled her coat tighter around her as the cool spring air fluttered her dress.

Martina was still thinking about her gift as she helped her family clean up after dinner. What a brilliant, unusual man Mr. Willoughby had been. He was the only person Martina ever met who had a magical element about him, something she couldn't explain. She had always categorized things as either real-life or make-believe, her reality or books, with nothing crossing the barrier, except for him. His stories were obviously myth, but he told them as his own experiences. That was what she was sure she would miss the most. But even though Mr. Willoughby was gone, at least she now had a good way to remember him.

Finding a spot for the music box was easy. Martina placed it on her nightstand beside the lamp and the book she was going to start reading first thing tomorrow. That night, as she waited to fall asleep and dream about the whole summer stretched out before her, she listened to the melody that the music box played. Sleepily, she watched as Mr. Willoughby made trip after trip around the miniature ice cream shop until her lids finally drooped, and she slept soundly.

Chapter 2 - The Secret Door

"Brrrraaaaaaaaaaaaaaaaaawpblblblblbl!
Braawpt! Braawpt! Glglglglglglglglgl!"

Martina's morning did not begin as musically as the night before had ended. She leaned out the window and glared at her friend for waking her.

"How do you like my song?" Heath asked

Her best friend—and luckily, next-door neighbor—was prancing through her yard wearing nothing but a red swimming suit and a shiny brass tuba.

"It's so thoughtful of you to be my alarm clock," she muttered. But how could she possibly stay mad at Heath?

"Put on your bathing suit, Martina," Heath said. "We're going to my pool!" He blared his tuba again.

Martina turned away from the window and rushed through changing and brushing her teeth. Running out the side door, she twisted her hair into a bun. She chomped on the breakfast bar she had grabbed on her way through the kitchen. As Martina emerged from the house, Heath was still talking to her mother as she weeded the flowerbed.

"And then I want the tubas to roar like lions," Heath said. "Like this: Roooooooooar," He roared through his tuba.

Martina noticed that Mom tried not to laugh.

"That's wonderful, Heath," Mom replied. "I can't wait to hear it when it's completed."

"When what's completed?" Martina asked.

"My *Tubas of the Jungle Opera*!" Heath replied, as if Martina should have known. He made another horrible squawking sound with his tuba, probably believing it to be a perfect animal imitation.

"What's *Tubas of the Jung*—" Martina began.

"I'm writing it!" Heath announced. "And you will be the second person ever to hear all my great ideas for it. Just come on. I'll tell you on the way to the pool." He grabbed Martina's arm and began dragging her toward his backyard.

"Be back for lunch, hon," Mom called after them. "And put some sunscreen on. You don't want to burn on the first day of summer."

As Heath tooted his tuba through the two yards, Martina marched along behind him. Luckily, the house across from Martina's was for sale and empty, so that was one family who would not bear witness to Heath's charade.

"After the wild tuba beast leaps from the shadows," Heath crouched and then sprang forward, "the tuba prey screams in horror. Braawlwlwlwlwl."

Nearing the pool, Heath acted out other scenes from the opera while Martina hugged her sides to keep from falling over with laughter.

"That will be so great, I'm sure," Martina gasped out. "So where does the *musical* part come in?"

"Are you saying that my work isn't musical?" Heath exclaimed in both a mock Australian accent and mock horror, glaring at her as he approached.

This, of course, brought more laughter from Martina.

Halting, Heath stared at her. "Actually, I plan on doing a mixture of lyrical lines in two-part tuba harmony along with the jungle sounds produced by tubas accompanied by bongo drums! Is that what you wanted to hear?" He had likely grown tired of the accent and dropped it.

"Yeah, that is what I was looking for, thank you," Martina smiled at him as they arrived at the pool in Heath's backyard.

"Ah, now we swim!" he said. And with that, he pushed Martina into the pool.

"Hey!" Martina gurgled as she pushed her wet hair out of her face, while Heath returned to blasting his tuba at her. This time it actually sounded just like an elephant.

"Don't play that thing constantly, or you'll get sick of it like we are," Heath's oldest sister, Helena, moaned from the back door.

Heath and Martina looked at each other and laughed.

"How can she understand the needs of a musician?" Heath said.

Martina knew that Heath was looking forward to his first band camp later that summer, right before his freshman year. He told her before that he needed to make a good impression to get a good chair, and that meant playing his tuba as much as possible.

Because Heath's family consisted of himself, his mother, and his three older sisters, Helena, Harper, and Haley—all girls and non-musicians—he always told Martina, "I'm used to being misunderstood. Artists must sacrifice for their work."

"Mom said," Helena told Heath.

"Mom said," Heath mocked as he placed his tuba on one of the lounge chairs. As much fun as summer is supposed to be, it was always better for Heath when Helena went back to college in the fall. In fact, this year, Harper would be joining her.

Heath stretched his gangly arms and legs as he applied sunscreen on them. "I'm so buff I'm afraid I might burst the bottle." He pretended to flex as he squirted sunscreen on his other arm. His sandy blonde hair curled aimlessly, sticking out all over his head. "It's a good thing I shaved this morning," he said, applying sunscreen to his naturally hair-free jaw line.

"Yes. You are soooooo buff, and usually so hairy." Martina climbed out of the pool, dried off, and joined him in smearing on the sunscreen. "So, why do you have this new toy?" She pointed at the instrument gleaming in the sun. "I thought they didn't let you take the high school tubas over the summer."

"Well, I told my mom it would be so cool if I had my own tuba," Heath said, "and she made a deal with me. If I got all 'As' in eighth grade, she would get me one."

Martina's jaw dropped. "So she bought you your own tuba? That's so cool!"

"Well, kind of," Heath said. "I know she didn't think I could do it. That's why she cut the deal with me. But I proved her wrong." He puffed up his chest and threw his head back with a cocky smile.

Martina took a closer look at the tuba and noticed some of the lacquer was gone from around the valves. "Did your mom buy it used?"

"It was my father's tuba," Heath answered, "but it's still in good shape. I had no idea she still had it until she gave it to me."

"I wonder why she didn't give it to you sooner."

"You know my mom." Heath frowned. "I don't think she was planning on giving it to me at all. I'm not like my perfect sisters." He jerked his thumb toward the house. "By the way, I overheard her talking to the witches' council earlier, and they were thinking about going shopping today. Do you think your family would care if I hung out at your house?" Heath put on a dramatic puppy-dog face.

"Doubt they'd care," Martina said. "My parents like you at least as much as they like that mutant they claim is my brother." The pair had always been inseparable, and they hung out at Martina's house so often that her parents jokingly counted Heath as one of their children. He even kept his Tiger Warriors sleeping bag at her house when they were in elementary school.

Martina glanced over at Teagan's bedroom window where he had placed a collection of robot warriors. He knocked them out into the yard, only to race down the stairs, pick them up, and carry them back to his room again. Martina wished she could trade her real brother for Heath.

"I don't think I ever did stuff like that when I was little." Heath scratched his head, watching the toys clatter together on the ground.

"No, you didn't," Martina said. "You were normal. And you never put Play-doh in my hair either." She snapped the lid shut on the sunscreen and set it on the ground, laughing. "I just don't understand why my parents have to be so compassionate."

"I think there's a law about it," Heath replied. He watched Teagan play for a moment. "So, what did you think of the funeral yesterday?"

"It was about the same as any other funeral. Have you ever been to one?" She regretted saying that as soon as the words left her mouth. When he was three years old, Heath's father passed away when he wrecked his car during a snowstorm. Because he had been so young, Heath told Martina he didn't remember much about his father.

When Heath glanced at his tuba, Martina felt even worse. His father had played tuba as a hobby, which was one of Heath's memories of him. He would sit on his father's lap and "help" press the keys, the deep blaring of the horn thrilling Heath even at such a young age.

"I'm sorry. I wasn't thinking."

"It's okay," Heath said.

"Hey, I did want to tell you that London stopped by last night," Martina said. She waited for Heath to ask why. The two of them enjoyed playing the "I know something you don't know" game, making the other person ask questions.

"London Bridge?"

"No, Mr. Willoughby's great-granddaughter. She —"

"Right, right. She stopped by?"

Martina explained about the box and the gifts. Heath looked perplexed.

"So you were in his will?" Heath asked.

"Not really," Martina said. "It was just the watch and a music box. Nothing as important as the note made it sound. But my music box is so cool! It looks just like Mr. Willoughby and the shop."

"It sounds pretty cool," Heath said. "Will you show it to me?" He walked over to the pool and jumped in, splashing Martina and ending their conversation.

Not to be outdone, Martina jumped in too, and they took turns trying to dunk each other.

"Hey, I can't hold my breath that long," Martina gasped. "You know that."

"You should really take up tuba," Heath said. He shook his head and feigned pity. "I have lungs of steel. I can probably hold my breath like five minutes."

Martina gave him a good dunk just to see.

A little before noon, Heath's mother stuck her head out the patio door. "Hi, Martina. We're all going to the mall. Would your parents let Heath stay with you today?" she asked sweetly.

"I don't think they'll care," Martina responded.

"Oh, good. Tell them 'thank you' for me," Dr. Melody Baldric, Heath's mom, said. "Heath, why don't you pack a change of clothes and anything else you'll need today." She retreated as quickly as she had come.

Heath climbed out of the pool sighing, making a big deal of drying off, and headed inside.

Martina stayed in the pool to keep from getting cold while waiting for him.

After a few minutes, Heath returned with a duffel bag. He threw his tuba over one shoulder and waited while Martina dried off. "She didn't even ask me to go with them." He scuffed his feet on the concrete around the pool.

"Did you really want to go?" Martina replied. "Wouldn't you rather hang out with me?" She wondered why Heath's mother was so rude all the time.

"Eh, I would rather hang out at your house, but it'd still be nice to be given an option," Heath said. The two of them made the trek back to Martina's house and ventured inside. Mom was standing at the dining room table sorting the mail into piles.

"How was the swim?" Mom said. She glanced at Heath's duffel bag. "Oh, do we get you already this summer, Heath?"

"If it's okay with you," Heath replied. "My mom's taking the three little pigs to the mall." He shrugged.

"Heath, that's not nice to say about your sisters," Mom said. "You know where the guest bedroom is, and there are extra bath towels in the hall closet." She smiled at them as Heath headed up the stairs.

"Mom, why is his family so mean to him?" Martina asked. "It's like they hate him."

"Oh, Martina, they don't hate him," Mom replied. "It's just difficult for them to find things to do together. Brothers and sisters don't always get along as well as you and Teagan do." She gave Martina a hug and kissed her forehead.

Martina wasn't sure what else to say.

*   *   *   *   *   *

Once Heath and Martina had both showered and eaten lunch, they were left on their own again. They went out on the front porch and sat in the swing so they could talk about everything that had happened at school, because they hadn't talked much that week. With the impending summer vacation, Heath had been taking extra tuba lessons after school, and both Martina and Heath had been spending their evenings studying for final exams.

"I heard that Lila Cadwalder is going to be the drum major this year," Heath said. "I don't think I'll be able to take my eyes off of her to look at the music. That's going to make band camp so awesome."

"Maybe you could memorize all your music. Then you won't have to worry about it," Martina said, half serious.

Heath stroked his hairless chin, apparently considering the possibilities.

Martina made a face as the thought of Heath gazing adoringly at Lila turned her stomach. Gross!

"Hey," Heath said. "Weren't you going to show me that music box Mr. Willoughby gave you?"

"Oh, yeah, I forgot," Martina said. "It's on my nightstand. Come on." She slid off the swing and put her sandals back on. They went inside and ran up the stairs to Martina's room.

Upon reaching the table, Martina gently picked up the box and held it out so Heath could see it. His eyes lit up as he asked her what song it played.

"I don't really know." She opened the lid and wound the key on the back.

Now, Heath could see the scene inside. "That thing is so cool."

Mr. Willoughby came through the door and slid around to the ice cream machine.

"It really looks like him," Heath said.

Upon arriving at the machine, the handles all flipped, and the front of the machine opened.

"Where did he get it?"

"I have no idea," Martina answered.

The tiny Willoughby continued through the ice cream machine and began the trek through the door and around again while the music played in the background.

"That song sounds so familiar." Heath stuck his ear about an inch from the box. "Does that sound like a cello?"

"Might be."

"Maybe old Mr. Willoughby wrote the music and paid someone to make the box," Heath said. "And he wants me to write it for the high school marching band so both of us can be famous."

Martina swore she saw dollar signs flash through his eyes. "I can't imagine that's what he wanted. If it were, then why would he have given Teagan a broken watch?" she challenged.

"Maybe the watch is a metronome," Heath said. "You turn the dial to set the speed, and it also tells time . . . and stuff." He started to run out of steam.

"I give up," Martina said. "I guess you win. The music box is for you to make money, and the watch is a metronome for you. The only problem is . . . THE GIFTS WERE CLEARLY FOR ME AND MY BROTHER." She rolled her eyes and set the music box down. Then, she plopped onto her bed and turned on the TV. As she flipped channels, she quickly skipped past a piece on the news saying that southern Asia was still flooding.

Heath sank into Martina's desk chair. "I know I recognize that song." Heath frowned.

Martina rolled onto her back and stared at the ceiling. "Just give it up," she said. "There is nothing to figure out. He just thought the box would be a reminder of how thankful he is that we took over the shop for him."

Heath didn't seem satisfied with that explanation. "Maybe he wants your family to hire me to play tuba every evening at the ice cream shop! I could serenade the customers just like people in fancy restaurants do with piano players and string quartets. That would be the best thing ever. I'd be famous! Maybe Lila would notice me then." Heath daydreamed.

Martina wanted to bring him back to reality. "That's the craziest thing I've ever heard you say," she said.

Heath looked at her, crestfallen.

"I don't think that's what he had in mind," Martina said, "because people usually talk while they eat, so they wouldn't be listening to your music, anyway."

"I give up then," Heath said. He tipped the chair back on two legs and rested against the wall.

"I think some mind-numbing cartoons will take care of any more thinking for the day," Martina stated as she flipped through the channels.

For the next twenty minutes, the Scary Ugly Combat Monsters entertained them with another episode of hunting down and destroying all the villains they could find. As the end of the show approached, the Monsters finally found the last evil-doer as they pulled a lever hidden on the outside of a garage. It caused the garage to turn upside down and reveal a hidden evil laboratory.

Heath gasped.

"It's just a TV show. Everything will be okay," Martina said. "All the Scary Ugly Combat Monsters will be back tomorrow to save the world before dinner time."

"No, no, no! I just figured it out," Heath said. "What if the music box isn't just a music box? What if it's a clue telling us where some evil laboratory, or something, is hidden?" As he spoke, his eyes grew enormous. He sat up in the chair so fast it almost tipped over.

"What—like Mr. Willoughby had a secret lab he wants us to find?" Martina replied skeptically.

"Come on, Martina," Heath said.

"So you think if we can figure out what song that is," Martina began, "then we'll know what the words to the song are. And they will tell us where the, um, 'secret evil lab' is located, Tuba Boy? That's *got* to be the craziest thing you ever said." She tossed a pillow at him and turned back to the Scary Ugly Combat Monsters as they beat the bad guys and sent them to jail.

"No, I didn't say that. You did. So *you* are the crazy one," Heath said. "I'm saying, what if the music box is *showing* us where the lab or whatever is hidden, not *telling* us?" Heath strode over to the nightstand and picked up the box. He wound the key and set it back on the table.

"Look." With his index finger, Heath followed the path of the minuscule Mr. Willoughby. "First he comes through the door from the house, and then he crosses to the ice cream machine." As Heath narrated, the figure did exactly that. "Then the handles all flip to the left. And now the front of the machine opens, and he goes inside." Heath looked back at Martina for a sign of confirmation.

"And then he goes back through to the other door and does it again," Martina said. "Apparently the person who made this music box had as much imagination as you do." She stared at Heath, a smile tugging the corner of her mouth. "You watch too many movies."

"But, you read all those books where this stuff happens," Heath challenged. "What if I'm right?"

"Heath, that's the thing," Martina said. "That stuff only happens in books and movies. It doesn't happen in real life. Besides, you can't be right, because that machine doesn't open that way. And if it did, my family would have figured it out in the last ten years that we have been living here!" She was sure she was correct.

Heath began pacing. "But your family doesn't turn all the handles to the left at once, do they?"

"Of course not!" Martina replied. "That would cause the vanilla, chocolate, and swirl to ooze at the same time. Ice cream would squirt out all over the floor. Besides, even if the machine did open like that, the 'entrance' wouldn't go anywhere because there's a wall on the other side of that machine." She crossed her arms, challenging Heath to argue back.

"But have you ever tried it?" Heath whispered.

"No, because all the ice cream would spill out of the machine and—" Martina began.

"But you can't say that for sure because you haven't tried it," Heath said.

"No, but we know what would happen, so why would we try it?" Martina felt exhausted from the long argument.

"Because there's a hidden door there! That's why you would try it." Heath gestured toward the ice cream shop. "I wonder what's hidden back there. Maybe a treasure! Or maybe it's a lab where Mr. Willoughby was making something top secret before he sold the place!"

Heath was beginning to sound crazy again.

Martina felt she needed to stop him. "First of all, if—I am saying 'if'—if there is a secret passageway, there is definitely no space for a hidden room, okay?"

"Okay," Heath said. "But there is room for a treasure, right?"

"There might be. But definitely not an entire room."

"So, all we have to do is flip the handles and go in." Heath grabbed Martina's arm, pulled her off the bed, and headed for the door.

"Wait! We can't try it right now," Martina hissed. "The shop is open, and Mom and Aunt Cassie are in there with all the customers. If they see us do open the ice cream machine and there is a treasure, then people will be bugging us all the time to see it." She dug her heels into the floor to stop Heath. "And, if we do it and there is no treasure, we'll spend the rest of the day cleaning up the ice cream we spilled."

"Okay. So we just have to wait until no one is around." Heath let go of Martina's arm and started pacing again.

"The shop doesn't close until eight, and then they have to clean up," Martina said. "If we wander in and flip the handles, they'll wonder what we're doing." As she paused to breathe, Heath opened his mouth to speak, but Martina cut him off. "So let's just forget about it."

"How can you ignore a hidden passageway? Mr. Willoughby obviously wanted *you* to find it, or he wouldn't have sent you the music box, right?"

Martina had to admit, Heath had piqued her interest. After a minute she answered. "Okay. You *might* be right," She said. She collapsed on the bed again and propped her head on her hands. "But how do you think we should do this?"

"We have to do what they do on TV: wait until everyone's asleep," Heath stated.

"I don't think so," Martina said. "I am not sneaking around while my parents are asleep. They would kill me if they found out. And they will anyway, if there is a pile of ice cream on the floor tonight."

"Fine, I'll go myself." Heath walked downstairs, ending the conversation.

Martina followed, hoping the subject would be forgotten over dinner.

*   *   *   *   *   *

Around nine o'clock, Teagan was in bed, and Mom and Dad took sodas out on the back porch like they usually did when the weather was nice. Martina was glad to see they were cooperating with her plan. She had managed to convince Heath that sneaking into the shop while they were outside was a much better idea than waiting until they were asleep.

"Awesome. We won't have to wait so long that way," Heath grinned.

The pair was at the dining room table, engrossed in a thousand-piece puzzle of a beach at sunset when the parents went outside.

A few minutes later, Heath pushed back his chair and stood up. "Are you ready?" he whispered.

"I guess so. I'm going to smack you if you're wrong, though. Just keep that in mind."

"I'm not wrong, so you won't have to worry about it." Heath smiled and turned toward the door to the shop.

They crossed the dining room and opened the door just far enough to go in. Martina punched in the security code on the keypad by the door to shut off the camera that videoed the store all night.

As they slid through the crack, the door creaked, and they held their breaths. Martina glanced nervously back at the patio door, but her parents were completely oblivious.

"No lights," Heath hissed as Martina reached for the switch. "We have to be stealth."

Martina stopped abruptly. "I'm not going if I can't see. I'll get a flashlight." Maybe they wouldn't be able to try Heath's idea after all. Darn.

"Already got one." Heath pulled a small flashlight out of his pocket and turned it on. "I grabbed this from your desk. I hope you don't mind."

"Oh, no," Martina said. "It's all right if you go through my desk whenever you want to, Klepto."

"Klepto! I love it." Heath chuckled.

The two of them crossed from the door to the ice cream machine where, in the music box, the miniature Willoughby had stopped. Heath shone the flashlight on the handles and took hold of the left one. Martina grabbed the right and middle handles.

"On the count of three. Ready? One, two, three," Heath counted.

They turned the handles simultaneously.

The machine made a sound like air rushing through a vent and began to vibrate. Martina stepped back, wrinkling her nose as the familiar sound of the ice cream pump started somewhere deep in the machine. Heath clenched his fists and waited.

"This is going to be bad," Martina whispered.

A loud thunk sounded from the spout, causing Martina to wince, thinking that any second, freezing ice cream would be shooting out of all three nozzles and end up in a huge lump on the shining floor.

However, ice cream did not pour from the machine. Instead, the front of the machine began to swing slowly outward, just as it had in the music box. When the door was completely open, all they could see was a small stairway spiraling into the darkness below.

Martina's eyes felt as big as bowling balls. She looked back and forth between Heath and the gaping hole, completely shocked. After her certainty that they would find themselves standing in a pile of ice cream, she had never considered that Heath might be right. All she could do was stare and back slowly away from the newly exposed entrance.

"Things are not always as they seem, eh?" Heath echoed the words from Mr. Willoughby's headstone. "Just like Mr. Willoughby used to say." He lightly punched Martina's arm and wiggled back and forth doing an "I'm right—you're wrong" dance. "Do you want to go first or should I?"

"I-I-I, uh, I'm not going," Martina stuttered.

"What do you mean you're not going?" Heath hissed. "Do you just want to stand there while I rush into an adventure?"

"We don't know what's down there!"

"Exactly. All the more reason to check it out. Now, are you going?"

"No. We *can't* go down there."

"Suit yourself. I'll let you know about the cool things I find when I get back. Maybe I'll even give you some of the treasure."

"You don't know there's a treasure, for sure."

"There has to be *something* good down there!" Heath flicked the light onto his face, grinning mischievously, and started down the stairs. He shined the flashlight through the passageway, but all Martina could see was the black metallic stairs glinting in the beam.

"He's really serious about this." Martina watched as he continued down the stairs, the light growing smaller. "What if he gets into trouble and needs help? I can't let him go alone," she thought. "And what if Mom and Dad ask where Heath is?" Cautiously, she poked her foot through the entryway, almost like she was testing cold pool water.

Holding her breath, Martina forced herself to follow Heath through the entrance. She had taken a few hesitant steps down the twisting staircase, when the door of the machine eerily closed behind them, grinding to a menacing halt that echoed in the cavernous depths, leading to who knows where.

Chapter 3 - Something Left Behind

The sound of the door clanking shut reverberated across the emptiness below them.

Martina gasped.

Heath spun around, shining the flashlight on the closed door. A large silver handle gave them hope that they weren't trapped.

Martina exhaled in relief.

"It looks like we'll be able to get back out," Heath said as he continued downward.

Gritting her teeth, Martina followed him down the metal spiraling stairway, wary of making any unnecessary sounds. Grasping the railing tightly, she became conscious of the squeaking of her tennis shoes on the slick stairs. As she trekked on into the darkness, she soon lost track of how far down they had gone.

Heath stopped abruptly, and Martina nearly crashed into him.

She barely breathed. "What is it?" she said close to his ear.

He didn't respond.

Heart pounding in her throat, Martina squeezed Heath's arm and strained her eyes to see in the darkness. He remained perfectly still. Finally, she felt his muscles relax. "What is it?" she whispered again, this time not so urgently.

"It sounds like water dripping." Heath started downward again.

"What did you think it was?" Martina wondered what he could have mistaken for dripping water.

"Footsteps," Heath replied nonchalantly.

For the next couple minutes, Martina tried to convince herself that Heath's overactive imagination and desire to add excitement to their lives were getting the best of him.

Again, Heath stopped suddenly, but Martina was alert this time. The echo of the dripping water had grown slightly louder. She strained to hear. Then, Martina thought she heard what made Heath stop. Very faintly, the sound of children singing could be heard over the dripping. It was discordant and distant, making the words smear together. Maybe she was imagining the sounds.

Then Heath spoke up. "Can you hear . . . singing?"

"Um, oh, no," Martina said. "It must be the echo of the water dripping." It was as much to convince Heath as herself.

Several minutes went by before either spoke.

"Whatever it is, it's getting louder," Heath said.

"Let's go back. We've gone far enough." Martina stepped backward, aware of the crinkle noise her pants made.

"No way!" Heath said, a little louder than Martina would have liked. "We've come this far. I bet we're almost to the bottom already."

Now, the only sound Martina heard was the dripping of water. The singing had stopped. "I still think we should go back." She cautiously retreating a few stairs.

"Don't do that," Heath prodded. "We have to be close to finding whatever Mr. Willoughby wanted us to find." He wielded the one card that he knew would convince Martina to go on.

Biting her lip, Martina struggled with curiosity and fear. Was she willing to risk whatever was down there to find the treasure? Surely Mr. Willoughby wouldn't send her somewhere dangerous.

Taking a deep breath, Martina assented. "Maybe we should keep going, then, just a little further." She retraced the steps she had just hastily made back toward the flashlight.

"Let's move!" Heath said. "You're not going back up those stairs until we find whatever we are supposed to find." He stuck the flashlight directly in Martina's face.

Blinking away dots, Martina swatted the flashlight, knocking it from Heath's hand. The pair watched in horror as the flashlight flew over the railing and plummeted toward the ground. The spot of light shrank as the flashlight got closer to the floor, far below. Finally, it cracked into the ground and went out.

In complete darkness now, Martina and Heath scrambled back up the stairs. Blindly, they tripped over each other and the steps as they raced toward the exit.

Finally, Martina smacked into the door at the top and felt for the handle. Finding it, she twisted and pulled violently. It would not budge an inch. With the two of them pulling on it, the rusty fixture finally creaked open, and the front of the ice cream machine slowly swung outward.

Martina scampered across the ice cream shop to the door to the house with Heath close behind. Glancing back at the machine, she watched the door clang shut. There was no ice cream on the floor, nor any sign of their short-lived adventure.

Back inside the house, Martina and Heath collapsed at the dining room table. Both were breathing so hard they couldn't even talk for several minutes. Martina did a quick check outside. Her parents seemed oblivious that something extraordinary had just happened.

"I think whatever was in there heard us," Heath said.

"*I* think it heard *you*," Martina said. "You were so loud when you were talking. I know that's why it stopped singing. And then we dropped the flashlight, and I *know* it heard that."

"You knocked it out of my hand," Heath protested. "Wait. You heard the singing, too? I knew it."

"I'm not sure what I heard," Martina pouted. "It doesn't really matter, because whatever the sound was, if it was something alive, it knows we're here, now."

"But, it should have known that Mr. Willoughby had gone there too, right?" Heath asked. "And what was he doing wandering around there in the dark? Did you see any lights anywhere?"

"No, but we didn't look for them," Martina said. "But, it doesn't matter, because I'm never going back down there."

"I guess I'll be traveling solo, then, eh?" Heath tempted.

"You aren't going back down there either," Martina replied. "I'm not going to let you. It's dangerous. Besides, you were just as scared as me when we ran out of there. Why would you go back?"

"I wasn't scared," Heath said. "I just knew that you were and didn't want you to worry about me. So anyway, who did Mr. Willoughby take with him?" He cut Martina off as she opened her mouth to retort. "If someone else was with him, he wouldn't have left you that music box. He would have left it for them."

"True, but you still can't go back down there," Martina said. "Something might be living in that cave or whatever it is, and we don't know if it's dangerous. What if it attacks you?"

"What if it's friendly or in trouble?" Heath responded.

"You're just trying to contradict me."

"How can anything that sings be harmful?" Heath said. "Just because they didn't all sing in the same *key* doesn't make them bad. Besides, I don't think Mr. Willoughby would send us somewhere dangerous, do you?"

She felt like Heath was reading her thoughts. "Fine. Go by yourself. Then when you get bitten and die, you can explain to your mom that some weird creature in the ice cream machine came after you for invading his territory."

"First of all, my mom won't care," Heath said. "Second of all, no one is going to believe that crazy story. And third, your clock is wrong." He pointed at the clock.

Martina turned to look. "No, that's right," she said. "My watch has the same time."

"I guess we weren't down there as long as I thought," Heath said. "I could have sworn we were on that stairway for a lot more than five minutes."

"I felt like that, too. I guess not though." Martina yawned and got up. "I'm going to bed. Come on, so I can let you out." Heath got up and grabbed his bag. Martina walked him to the door and watched as he walked across the lawns to his back door. As he let himself into his house, Martina locked her door and went up to bed.

*   *   *   *   *   *

The next morning, Martina crawled out of bed at a "reasonable" time. In preparation for the truck that would be coming with supplies for the ice cream shop, she threw on shorts and a t-shirt and went downstairs for breakfast. Showering would have been pointless because of all the heavy boxes she would have to help haul in and stock. By the time she had brushed her teeth, the truck was pulling into the driveway.

Martina met her parents in the driveway and began unloading boxes. Just like two weeks ago, when everything was out of the truck, one box of mix was missing.

"I don't understand it," Dad said to the driver. "Every time we unload the truck, one box is always missing. The invoice says they loaded the right amount at the warehouse."

"I just drive the truck, man. I don't load it. You have to take that up with the company." The driver hopped back into the truck and drove off.

*   *   *   *   *   *

That afternoon, Martina was working with her mom and Aunt Cassie in the ice cream shop. Because it was the beginning of summer and not a particularly warm day, they did not have many customers, so Martina spent a lot of time thinking. What exactly was at the bottom of that exceedingly long stairway? What was eerily singing in there? And, what was it that Mr. Willoughby wanted her to find?

None of these questions could be answered, though, without making another trip down that stairway. Common sense was telling her that she shouldn't go back through the ice cream machine. However, Mr. Willoughby had obviously found something important that he wanted her to know about. But what could it be?

As she flipped the handle to squirt vanilla ice cream into a cone, she realized something. Maybe Mr. Willoughby had hidden some books at the bottom of the steps. She always loved reading, and Mr.

Willoughby had lent her so many books. And he was always giving her puzzles and riddles to solve. Maybe he left her a sort of scavenger hunt to lead her to the books. That sounded like something he would do. Shortly before he died, he had promised to lend her *The Mystery of Diamond Lake*, a story that takes place at the lake near Starry Fields High School, just a few blocks away. He certainly wouldn't send her somewhere scary to find these books.

That was all it took to give her courage. She would have to tell Heath that she wanted to go back.

Around four o'clock, Heath wandered into the shop.

"What can we get you, Heath?" Mom said.

"I'll take a banana split with peanuts and pineapple . . . and gummy worms! Thanks!" Heath waved at Martina and sat down at his favorite table.

"Hon, why don't you make yourself something, and quit for the day," Mom said to Martina. "I don't think we'll have many more customers."

Mom made Heath's dessert, while Martina made herself a hot fudge sundae. Then Martina brought both treats back to the table and sat down.

"Just the way I like it! Lots of gooey shtuff!" Heath announced, cramming in a huge mouthful of ice cream, dripping with pineapple juice. A gummy worm hung out of his mouth.

Martina held back from telling him just how nasty that was. Instead she leaned forward, making sure her aunt and mother couldn't hear. They were both making sundaes for themselves. Aunt Cassie was talking animatedly, waving her arms and laughing loudly.

"I want to go back," Martina said.

"Back where?" Heath asked, still stuffing his mouth full of banana split.

"You know." Martina jerked her head toward the ice cream machine.

"Oh, back to the house." Heath nodded toward the adults. "Sorry, don't kick me! I do know, okay." He swung his legs around to the side of the table to avoid being pummeled again. "What made you change your mind?" he whispered.

"I think that Mr. Willoughby wanted to leave me a puzzle so I would find his books."

"Why wouldn't he have just left them somewhere you could find them?" Heath said. "I think he's leading you to something too big to just leave lying around." He gasped, nearly choking on a peanut.

Martina had to wait for the coughing to subside to find out why.

"I bet it's an elephant!" Heath said.

"Heath, no. That's ridiculous," Martina began. But she was too late. Heath had already revved up his imagination.

"That has to be it," he said. "Mr. Willoughby was always trying new things, right? He wanted to combine different flavors in the shakes, and he invented multi-colored sprinkles."

Martina shot him a skeptical look.

"Okay, so he didn't invent them. But, he did start providing them in the shakes, too. And people called him crazy, but all his cool new ideas worked."

Heath waved his spoon in the air. "So, I think he was raising elephants down there and was using their milk to make ice cream instead of cow's milk. And now he needs someone to look after the elephants for him."

"Don't even make me tell you all the flaws in that story." Martina laughed.

When they had finished eating, they threw their plastic dishes and spoons in the big trash can by the door and went back in the house.

"I'm sure Mr. Willoughby wouldn't be raising elephants down there and then leave them without food while I try to figure out what's under the ice cream shop," Martina said.

"Good point," Heath said. "Maybe your music box shows what it is?" He sounded excited. "Let's look at it again. I want to listen to the music anyway. I think that might help. At least, it might be inspiring."

"I didn't know your imagination needed inspiration." Martina and Heath jogged up the stairs to Martina's room again. "We can listen, but I don't think you're going to recognize that song. It sounds . . . different."

Heath ran to the nightstand. As he grabbed the box, a panel on the front of the box popped off and landed on the floor.

"You broke it, you klutz!" Martina snatched the box from Heath's hand and inspected it. As she did, a scrap of newspaper fluttered to the ground.

"I don't think I broke it," Heath protested. "That was supposed to come out."

When Martina turned the box upside down, she could see the spring mechanism that Heath had triggered when he picked up the box. She tipped the box back for a better look, and she could see a small hollow space where the paper had been.

After setting the box down, Martina picked up the paper and unfolded it. It was a very old, yellowed picture of Mr. Willoughby and another man wearing tunics and pants with funny hats. "Must have been a costume party," she said. Printed on the back in Mr. Willoughby's rough handwriting was one line only: "Something I've left behind me: 12-24-36."

"What's that supposed to mean?" Heath leaned over Martina's shoulder to read the note again.

"I have no idea," Martina said. "What was Mr. Willoughby doing on December twenty-fourth, 1936?"

"Hmmm, that's Christmas Eve," Heath pondered. "Or maybe that's someone's birthday?"

"But why would that be something he 'left behind' him?" Martina asked.

"Maybe he forgot someone's birthday and regretted it," Heath suggested. "Or he didn't like the last-minute Christmas shopping that year."

"You know who might know?"

Heath shrugged.

"London."

"London Bridge?" Heath grinned.

Martina rolled her eyes. "Let me call her and see if we can stop by." She dialed London's number.

*   *   *   *   *   *

Half an hour later, they found themselves seated in London's den sipping lemonade that her mother had brought them.

Martina and Heath watched London intently. She was wearing her favorite swim team shirt, one that Martina also loved, that said "Of course girls like butterflies." For the fortieth time, Martina watched London run her fingers through her platinum blonde hair, apparently hoping the scalp massage would bring memories back to the surface. Finally, London leaned forward in her chair.

"Do you remember anything?" Martina prodded.

"I have no idea what happened on that date," London gestured at the photo.

"Did he ever mention anything important that happened a long time ago?" Heath said.

"Nothing I can remember, but we could look at some of his pictures," London answered. "Maybe we'll find one from this costume party. They're over here." She approached the stack of old photo albums on the bottom shelf of the cabinet, just below a shelf full of her swimming trophies and medals. Kneeling, she shoved her book bag over to make room for the others to sit down. The three began to flip through the sepia-toned pictures.

Finally Martina spoke up. "I don't think this is going to help. I mean, none of the pictures are labeled, so we don't even know what year they're from." Martina leaned back and put her hand right on top of London's lock from her school locker. It must have fallen out of her book bag. "Ow." Picking it up, she absentmindedly twisted the lock in her hands.

"Should we ask my dad?" London said. "He might know. But he's probably too involved in his cases to pay attention to stuff like this." London's father, Mr. Willoughby's grandson, Ian, was a popular lawyer, one from the commercials, who spent most of his time at the office.

Heath shrugged, and Martina continued to toy with the lock, staring at it as if it would give her the answer. Suddenly, she stopped. Holding the lock up in the air, she grinned widely at her friends.

"Will you please talk," Heath gently shook Martina's shoulders.

"This lock!" Martina said. "Don't you see? Look at the numbers on it." The others stared at her as if she had lost her mind until recognition finally dawned on their faces.

"I get it," London said. "Maybe it's not a date but a lock combination."

"That's so cool," Heath said. "Mr. Willoughby left you a lock combination. What a weird thing to give someone." Heath started laughing.

"That means there has to be a lock somewhere," Martina said.

London picked up the picture off the floor and looked at it again.

Heath stopped laughing. "Oh, I thought he just left you a lock combination. I really want to do that to someone now."

"No," Martina said punching him lightly in the stomach.

Heath curled up and pretended to block punches with his arms.

"I wonder," London began.

"Wonder what?" Heath invaded London's personal space and opened his eyes wide.

London stood and began pacing. "I wonder if the safe is the one that's in the storage room at the Sundae Best."

"There's no safe in there." Martina shook her head.

"When I was little, I remember Great-Granddad sitting on his bed one time, looking at something," London said. "And he was talking to himself, saying that something would be okay in the safe in the storage room." She looked like she was thinking hard. "I asked him what he meant, but he just said the same thing it says here: 'something I left behind me.' I didn't remember that until you reminded me with the lock."

"So we just have to find the safe and open it, right?" Heath asked.

"I don't know exactly where the safe *is*, though," London replied.

"But there can't be a safe there," Martina protested. "I've never seen one."

"Maybe it's hidden somewhere," London said. "Can we go look for it now? I'm so excited to see what Great-Granddad left you!"

"What did he leave you, London?" Heath asked.

"Some awesome, old movie paraphernalia—posters, soundtracks, piano music—a whole box full of cool stuff," London said.

"Maybe I could play some of it for you on my tuba." Heath puffed his chest up proudly.

"Yeah, that would be cool," London said. "So, Martina, can we look for the safe?"

"Sure," Martina said. "But we'll have to make up an excuse about what we're doing in the storage room. We aren't normally allowed in there."

"Tell your mom you think you left something there this morning when you were unloading the boxes," Heath said. "Then when we come back out, tell her you must have left it somewhere else."

"Okay. Let's go then." Martina jumped up and headed for the door.

Upon entering the ice cream shop, Martina told her mom that they were going to look for a hair band she thought she had dropped that morning when they were moving boxes.

"Sure, hon," Mom said.

Aunt Cassie smiled. She had recently decided to chop off her long hair, which Martina had so adored, and was showing Mom the pictures in the magazine that inspired the transformation.

Upon entering the storage room, Martina, Heath, and London shut the door and stared at the mountain of boxes.

"How are we going to find anything in here?" London asked.

"If we move the boxes out from the wall one at a time, I'm sure we can find it," Martina said. "The only things that have always been in here are the desk, the walls, and the carpet. I bet there's a secret button or hidden handle somewhere like in the Terezia Snow mysteries." She walked toward a small stack of boxes near the wall and attempted to move them.

"What about this?" London said. "Has it always been here?" She rushed over to a painting that was partially concealed by a stack of boxes.

"Yeah, it was here ever since I was little," Martina said. "Let's take a look." She raced over to London to help her move the boxes. Heath wedged himself between the boxes and the wall, and the three of them managed to shove them out far enough to examine the painting.

"That's Mr. Willoughby!" Martina pointed at the painting. "And the paper says something he left behind him. Do you think that means behind a picture of him?"

"Let's find out." Heath took hold of both sides of the picture and gently lifted it off the wall. Behind it was a safe door exactly the same size as the framed picture. "London, you've got the numbers."

"Here, Martina. He left this for you," London said.

Safely hidden behind the boxes, the three of them held their breath as Martina began to turn the lock.

"Just like my school locker," Martina thought. First, she cleared it by turning it several times to the right. Then she stopped on twelve. Turning it back to the left, she passed twelve and stopped at twenty-four. Finally, she turned it back to the right directly to thirty-six. When she stopped moving the dial, a soft click echoed inside the safe. Martina looked at Heath and London excitedly. She firmly grabbed the handle and pulled the safe door open.

Chapter 4 - Fire, Water, and Air

In the darkness, Martina could barely see something glinting at the back of the safe. "What's that?" She reached for the glittery object.

When she pulled her hand out, Martina was holding three bejeweled keys on leather straps. Each strap was blackened with age, but the jewels on the keys shown brightly. The keys looked exactly like old-fashioned wrought iron house keys with perfectly round jewels set in the handles. The smooth gems sparkled vividly, the insides swirling with a cloudy material like diamond dust. Carved onto the shaft of each key was a single word. The key with the red jewel bore the word "Fire," the blue jewel, "Water," and the silver jewel, "Air." The handles were tinged with the same color as the stones.

They stared at their find.

"We should take them upstairs where no one will see us," Martina said.

She gave the keys to Heath, who dropped them into the cargo pocket on his shorts. They closed the safe and replaced the painting and boxes, making sure that the room looked exactly as they had found it.

Quickly, Martina headed for her room muttering, something to the adults about looking elsewhere for her hair band as Heath and London followed. Once upstairs, Martina locked her door and turned on the TV so no one could hear them.

Heath laid the keys out on Martina's bed.

"What could these possibly go to?" London asked. She picked one up and examined it. "I wonder why Great-Granddad kept them in the safe."

Martina and Heath looked at each other. Heath nodded to Martina.

"Well," Martina said, "we don't know what the keys go to, but we have an idea where it might be."

Martina and Heath told London about the music box and the ice cream machine, including a full account of their most recent discovery which led them to asking for her help.

"I can't believe it," London said. "Great-Granddad kept that ice cream machine a secret. It's just, wow. I have to go with you down the stairs."

Heath grinned at Martina.

"You can come," Martina said, "but you can't tell anyone about this. No parents, no friends, nobody. The three of us are the only ones who can know."

"I feel like we should pinky swear or do some sort of blood oath," Heath commented.

"Let's pinky swear," London said. Martina knew she was wrinkling her nose at the thought of blood.

Martina laughed. "This is such an elementary school way to seal a pact." She stuck out her pinky. "Are we sworn to secrecy?"

The three began planning for their next big trip through the ice cream machine with hopes that they would get a little farther this time.

"We have to wait until my parents and Teagan are busy away from the shop, since we have to get to the machine without them knowing," Martina said. "And Mom and Aunt Cassie are usually in the shop all day." Reluctantly, they decided to wait until that night.

*   *   *   *   *   *

The rest of the day was spent making preparations for their trip. They would be using the guise of a slumber party so London could stay late. Because Heath's mother didn't care what he did, he left a note saying that the Mackenzies were letting him hang out late. After renting movies from Rick's Flicks and making popcorn, they had set the scene to fool Martina's parents. To complete the effect, all three of them brought sleeping bags to the living room—Heath with his famous Tiger Warriors one—to lay on while they watched their movie. They began eating the popcorn and watching a tacky eighties horror flick.

All evening, the parents or Teagan were way too close for the crew to sneak back into the ice cream shop. At 8, Teagan went to bed. Finally, after what seemed like forever, Martina's parents headed for the stairs.

"Good night," Dad said. "Martina, make sure you turn the TV off when you girls finally go to sleep."

Martina, Heath, and London responded with a chorus of good nights, their heads propped against the couch in front of the TV.

After waiting about 30 minutes, Martina said, "Should we go?"

"I think everyone's asleep." Heath got up and walked over to the stairs to check for lights. "It's dark," he whispered. "I say we go. Let's synchronize our watches. The time on the mantle is 11:13."

"Right," Martina answered, though she didn't have on her watch.

Martina and London got up as well, and the three stuffed supplies they had hidden in their sleeping bags into Heath's backpack. Together, they had several flashlights, bottled water, and a mountain of snack crackers from Heath's cupboard.

"So who gets what key?" Heath said.

"Fire, water, air," London said as she pushed one toward each of them.

"Heath, I like the red one. Want to trade?" Martina asked.

"I gave them to you according to your zodiac signs." London grinned. "Leo, fire, Heath. Gemini, air, Martina. And Pisces, water, London."

"London has spoken. No trading." Heath shook his finger at Martina.

They each put a key around their necks and set off for Willoughby's Sundae Best.

Martina punched in the security code, and they crept through the door. A hollow metallic thunk behind her made her heart leap into her sinuses.

"Grrmph-gah," Heath articulated through clenched teeth as he motioned angrily toward the preparation counter, which must have purposely tripped him.

Cocking her head, Martina listened for her parents to race through the door and ground them all. She was met with silence.

They resumed creeping over to the machine. Heath and Martina turned the handles just as they had before. Martina smiled at London when she gasped, apparently surprised by the machine actually swinging open. Martina would be the first to admit that the story was a bit hard to swallow until you see it for yourself.

"Wow! This is so cool," London whispered.

"Flashlights on? Let's move." Heath took the lead, followed by the girls. After two steps, however, he stopped.

"Why'd you stop?" Martina said. The door clanged shut behind her.

"Is this thing glowing?" Heath pointed at the fire key around his neck.

"Yeah, it is!" Martina said. She pointed at Heath's key. "And it's pulling the cord tight." She reached toward him. "I mean, it's probably just caught on your shirt," Martina tried to disentangle the key from Heath's shirt. When she touched it, the glowing jewel felt hot. "Ow." The key was slowly rising into the air. She jerked her hand away, unable to believe what she was seeing.

They watched as the key rose and pulled tightly on the strap.

"Whoa, why's it doing that?" London started backing up the stairs.

"It wants me to follow it." Heath looked excited and punched his fist in the air. "Onward!"

Martina was finding it hard to keep her cool. "It's pointing up the stairs. I think it wants us to go back," she suggested, shakily.

"Do you guys have to make it sound like the key is alive?" London hissed. She wrung her hands.

Heath followed the key to the top step. But as he did so, the key slid on the string, pulling him just to the left of the door. He followed it, and the key pointed directly at the wall.

"Hey, look at this," Heath called. "There's a keyhole and a riddle. 'In the cave, it is dark as night. You will need fire to bring you light,'" Heath read.

"You're wearing the fire key," London exclaimed.

"I know." Heath grinned at the floating key.

"So try it," Martina said. "Maybe it will turn the lights on down there."

"Yeah, I wouldn't want you to drop your flashlight down the stairs again," Heath teased.

"*I* didn't drop the flashlight," Martina growled in response to Heath's quip.

Then, Heath took hold of the key and slipped it into the lock.

Suddenly, the stairway was illuminated with a bright orange light coming from under their feet.

"It looks like the stairs are on fire," Heath said.

"But all the fire is trapped under glass or something," London added.

"That's so cool," Heath said.

"I think it's creepy," Martina said. She hoped the fire wouldn't burn through the steps when they were halfway down. For all she knew, they might have just set off a security system. Since the others didn't look nervous, though, she decided to keep her mouth shut.

With the light from the fires, they could see their way down the stairs. But the rest of the room was still in complete darkness. The light from the flashlights was swallowed up, as if by a black hole.

"What kind of a weird place is this?" London asked.

"There is only one way to find out," Heath said. "We've got to get further than we did last night." Heath let the key drop back around his neck and started down the stairway again. "Let's go."

For several minutes, they descended in silence. Around and down, they went. The spiral stairway seemed to have no end. Suddenly, from the back of the group, London squealed just loud enough for them to hear.

They all stopped.

"Is that the singing you heard before?" She grabbed her friends excitedly.

They listened for a minute.

"That's the same sound alright," Heath said.

"It sounds like it's getting further away, though," Martina said. "Before, it was getting louder. I can barely hear it now." After a moment, she said, "I think it's gone."

"I want to find out what that is." Heath said.

Eventually, they neared the bottom of the stairway.

"Didn't it seem like we walked a lot longer last time, Heath?" Martina asked.

"Yeah, but we were going slower, because *someone* was a little scared." Heath tipped his head in Martina's direction. She slugged him.

At the bottom of the stairs, they faced a large, black, wooden door. A corridor stretched on into darkness both to the left and right of the door. Printed in neat gold letters on this door was the word "Entrance."

"Do you think this is the entrance?" Heath joked as he gestured toward the door like he was presenting letters on a game show.

"How will we ever know?" Martina asked in a ditzy voice.

"What are we *waiting* for?" London said. "I want to see what's on the other side."

Heath tried the knob on the door. "It's locked. The handle won't turn either way." He pulled on the handle and twisted it again, but it wouldn't budge. Squatting, he held the Fire key near the handle, but it remained motionless in his hand.

"Maybe we need a different key for this one," Martina said.

"There's something written above the handle." Heath shined his flashlight on it. "It's another riddle.

'In the open air is where you will be / When you use Air to open me.' It's pretty obvious what we need to do, but there's no keyhole."

"Odd." Martina frowned. "Maybe it doesn't mean the Air *key*."

Heath shrugged his shoulders. Filling his lungs like he was about to blast some fortissimo bass lines on his tuba, Heath puffed onto the doorknob. Then the doorknob was *wet* and locked.

"That's gross!" Martina stepped forward as London chuckled. She rolled her key back and forth between her fingers as she stared down the door. Martina didn't want the key to take on a life of its own as Heath's had but still felt excited to find out what was on the other side.

Pointing it toward the door, Martina took a few more steps. As she felt the warmth of the jewel in the handle of the key, part of her wanted to drop it. When she approached, Martina could feel the key pulling her directly toward the handle. She tried to ignore its power, scared to admit that it had any.

"I don't know where that key thinks you're going to put it," Heath said.

"Did you have to say that it 'thinks'?" Martina said. Finally, she took the key off her neck and held onto the jeweled handle. When the key was almost touching the handle, the handle molded like clay to produce a keyhole. "Whoa," she gasped.

Martina looked back at her friends and then slipped the key in the hole. It fit perfectly. She paused. What was she going to find? The situation had taken her far out of her comfort zone. She didn't like things that couldn't be explained. This trip was getting too weird for her. If she didn't open that door, though, one of her friends definitely would. Why was she the only one not enjoying this? She took a deep breath.

Turning the key, Martina pulled the heavy door open.

On the other side of the door was a room unlike any she had ever seen. It was long and dark and had a high, vaulted ceiling. The room was empty, except for two rows of columns on either side of a central aisle and large, blue, globe lanterns, which floated high above the floor like giant bubbles. In the dim light, the shadows from the columns danced from the bobbing and circling motions of the lanterns.

Heath and London peeked inside the door behind Martina. She turned and looked at them. Gesturing toward the room, she mouthed the words, "Keep going?" knowing what the answer would be.

The other two eagerly nodded.

Martina mustered enough courage to take one step and was followed quickly by Heath and London.

When she reached the first row of columns, Martina noticed three doors at the far end of the room. She started debating in her head which of them they should try first.

As she continued toward the center of the room, Martina stopped holding her breath. Her nagging fear that the blue bubbles would fall and crush them was apparently unfounded.

Suddenly, the heavy clank of metal echoed in the hall, startling her.

At that instant, warriors dressed in full armor and carrying swords, axes, and spears stepped from behind the columns.

Martina gasped.

London froze.

Heath finally stopped grinning. He swiveled his head, looking first at one and then another warrior.

These soldiers were about the same height as Martina and weren't very broad, but their weapons could slice through any opposition. The closest one approached them with sword drawn menacingly. It was a girl, her pale hair and face taking on an eerie glow from the blue lights.

Martina fought the urge to turn and run for the door.

"You are under arrest for trespassing in Sheardland," said the girl who approached them.

"We aren't trespassing," Heath said.

"All of you must come with me," the leader continued. "You will present yourselves in front of the Head Rhihalva, as it is his territory. He will decide your fate." As she spoke, she flexed her fingers around the sword handle, clearly ready to strike at any resistance. The others who moved in close behind her looked equally ready to lop the intruders' heads off.

"Please," Martina pleaded, "we were sent by someone who used to communicate with those who live here."

"Who is this you speak of?" The armed warrior maintained her stance.

"Mr. Willoughby," Martina said. "He left us clues about how to enter this place, so we thought we were supposed to come here." She looked at the others for support.

Heath was surprisingly silent, and London was now staring wildly around her and looking like she was going to cry.

"Ah, Mr. Willoughby," their captor responded. Her face betrayed no emotions.

Martina wasn't sure whether saying Mr. Willoughby's name was good or bad.

"You still need to see the Head Rhihalva," the warrior said. "Come with us." She turned and marched toward the end of the corridor.

There, a door was marked in a script that Martina couldn't read. She noticed how the eerie blue light reflected off the many piercings that studded the leader's pointed ears and wondered if she earned them from slaughtering her enemies.

With a deafening metallic clamor, the ranks of armor-clad soldiers surrounded them, making it certain they would not escape. The door swung open with the captain's touch.

Martina was shaking so badly she could barely walk. She wondered what would be on the other side of the door.

Emerging into the open air, Martina was astonished to find that they had entered a town that looked a lot like a town from hundreds of years ago. The building opened out onto a cobblestone street lined with shops. She looked back at the building they had just exited. There were windows outside it, though there were none inside. The sign above the front door said "Rhihalvberg Travel." "In English?" Martina thought. It was odd after the last sign she saw was written in a language she couldn't even recognize, much less read.

The main question in Martina's mind now was how they had exited at street level when they had clearly descended far below ground, down the long stairway inside the ice cream machine.

They ventured down the street behind their envoy, receiving strange looks from the people passing them, probably due to their clothes. The women they passed were wearing gowns. The men wore short tunics with pants, all in bright colors.

Heath caught Martina's eye and mouthed the words "nice pajamas," tipping his head toward some of the natives.

Martina gave him a look that plainly said "Shut up before you get us into more trouble." The outfits somehow looked familiar to her though. "From the picture of Mr. Willoughby in the music box," she thought. He had definitely ventured to this strange little town . . . wherever it was.

They continued past stores that sold flowers and animal parts, and stores where services included hair and talon cuts.

"Talon cuts?" Martina thought. "Like eagles, falcons, dragons?"

Farther down the street, a huge stone castle with three towers came into view. Arching from the roof in the center was a large glass bubble, much like an observatory.

Martina stared as she approached it, wondering what sort of doom they were being marched toward. The setting sun cast shadows around them, and the wind blew gently. So many questions swirled through Martina's mind now, as she stared at the world around her. She hadn't seen a single car. Had they gone through some kind of time warp in the bubble room? Was that even possible? Maybe this was like Brigadoon.

Approaching the building at the far end of the street, the group climbed the front steps. Two more warriors in full armor were standing on either side of the massive double-doors that marked the entrance to the building.

Martina glanced at Heath and London just long enough to catch the fear marked on their faces. Heath stared straight ahead, guarded—a look Martina had seen before when he was about to get in trouble at school. London was a bit more obvious. Her eyebrows were furrowed as she nibbled her lip.

The dark wooden doors gave off a sweet smell and were intricately carved with scenes from battles between a variety of odd creatures. Wondering if they would be victims to scenes such as these soon, Martina swallowed hard and patiently observed the captain.

The blonde warrior held her head high and approached the doors, and the two guards bowed to her and pulled them open. A sharp nudge in the back of her thigh told Martina she had no choice but to follow her captor inside. Heath and London entered with a couple more guards, while the rest of the army waited outside.

Martina thought the inside of this castle looked less like a medieval building and more like a Hollywood mansion, complete with a massive curved staircase that led to several doors above. Then, she turned and held back a shriek. In the nearby sitting room, two enormous creatures that reminded her of overgrown, hideous grey pigs wearing clothes were sharing cups of tea. Thankfully, Martina and her friends were led away from the tea party and toward a door just beyond the stairs.

Martina exhaled and looked over at Heath and London. They too looked relieved to be ushered elsewhere. Surely wherever they were going would be less creepy.

Once through the door, Martina found herself in a space that appeared to have no dimensions at all. A blinding whiteness was everywhere.

Then, the commanding officer spoke to them sternly. "Stay close to me or you may get lost out there." She gestured to the rest of the white space.

Confused, the three just nodded. No one's footsteps made any sound as they followed the warrior. They kept moving forward, and yet, their surroundings didn't seem to change.

"The Head Rhihalva is having some redecorating done." The warrior continued to march them through the emptiness.

They ventured across the white space in silence until the warrior stopped and opened an invisible door. As the door creaked open, the trio followed her into an enormous, but cozy chamber.

With the rows of books and big fireplace, Martina felt more at ease.

Across the room, sitting behind a large wooden desk, a man was reviewing a stack of documents. He stroked his beard, already flecked with silver hairs despite his apparent young age.

He frowned at the unexpected visitors and glanced toward the captain. Then he stood and brushed the wrinkles from his long black outfit. The small sign on his desk read, "Alfwyn Branimir, Head Rhihalva."

Chapter 5 - In the Head Rhihalva's Office

The warrior faced the Head Rhihalva. He stood, and they both held their right palms up at about shoulder level. Then, something very strange happened. They flexed their fingers and a small ripple of light flickered, touching both hands at once, as if in greeting.

"What brings you here so late today, Siofra?" the Head Rhihalva asked. He eyed the strangers suspiciously, then leaned on the front of his desk and looked expectantly at the warrior.

"We were alerted yesterday of a breach at Exit 248," Siofra said. "I moved the majority of the Alvar to this position and put them on high alert status. Today, we were notified of a further breach at Exit 248. This time, the breach continued to Exit 248B."

"248 is my house number," Martina thought. "Maybe using the fire key *did* set off an alarm."

"I moved my troops to the Blue room and waited for the trespassers there," Siofra continued. "They were not difficult to apprehend once they entered the area. All of them came quietly. This one claims that Mr. Willoughby sent them here." Siofra gestured toward Martina.

The Head Rhihalva nodded and maintained the stony look upon his face. "Mr. Willoughby, eh? I guess we should find out what they know." He sighed and approached them.

Martina was certain now that coming here had been a very bad idea.

Suddenly, the Head Rhihalva smiled at them. Calmly, he introduced himself and asked, "How exactly do you know Mr. Willoughby? How came you to enter our land?"

Martina looked at Heath, hoping for a nod of encouragement, but he was too busy staring at the huge fish tank in the middle of the room. She looked at London. London was eyeing Alfwyn suspiciously, like he was her competition at a swim meet. It didn't seem like either of her companions wanted to talk, so Martina knew she must say something.

"Heath and I are friends with Mr. Willoughby," Martina began, "and London is his great-granddaughter. I don't know if you knew, but he died recently. So I guess everything started with the music box he left me."

With a few interjections from Heath and London, Martina explained how they figured out exactly where the entrance was, how they got the keys that hung around their necks, and how they came to be in the same room as Alfwyn. When she finished explaining, Martina waited for his response.

"Siofra," Alfwyn said, "I think you will agree with me when I say we have nothing to worry about with these three."

"Yes, after hearing their story, I am certain that Mr. Willoughby has chosen wisely," Siofra said.

"His successors must be welcomed and revered." With that, she made a sweeping bow, her velvety plum cape swishing as she did so.

"His successors?" Martina, thought. "What does that mean?" She felt as though she could breathe easily for the first time and had overcome her fear somewhat, but she was still curious.

They all managed to bow stiffly in response and mustered nervous smiles.

Siofra turned to Alfwyn. "Do you wish me to leave, Sir?"

He nodded. "That will be all. Thank you."

Siofra spun around, her cape swirling behind her, and exited the room.

"Welcome to Adalborg," Alfwyn said. "That is the name of this house, where the Head Rhihalven have lived for centuries." He gave a small model of a carousel on his desk a spin. "I suppose we had better get started, then. Have you looked over the notes that Mr. Willoughby left you?"

"Notes?" Martina said. "We don't have notes. Just the music box and the keys."

"What's a Rhihalva?" Heath blurted out.

Alfwyn winked at him. "I suppose you have many questions, since you have read nothing about us and our culture. Why don't we have a seat over there?" Alfwyn walked quickly toward the side of the room behind the fish tank. He held out his hand and waved it in front of him. "Kathedra," Alfwyn said.

Instantly, four over-stuffed leather chairs appeared, clustered together as if they were deep in conversation. He walked over to them and sat down.

Martina stared at him, wondering how safe it would be to sit on something that had appeared out of thin air. Would it swallow her whole? Or would she fall straight through it onto the floor? Did she dare trust this man? Is he really a man at all? He seemed to know Mr. Willoughby, but still . . .

"How did you do that? That's so cool!" Heath exclaimed, recovering quickly from his shock. Before Martina could even voice her fears, Heath had leapt into one of the chairs, throwing his legs haphazardly over the arms. He sighed, put his arms behind his head, and grinned broadly at the girls.

Martina and London remained transfixed.

Alfwyn chuckled when he looked at Martina. "What's the matter? Leather not to your liking? I have always thought it quite sophisticated, myself. And the copy-cattle that it comes from are both useful and delicious."

"It's not that," Martina said. "It's just—"

"Is it safe?" London asked.

"Of course!" Afwyn said. "Do have a seat. Then I'll explain everything." He pointed to the other chairs.

The girls sat down but remained on the edge of the seats.

"First, let me address both of your questions, young man: What is a Rhihalva, and how did I do that?" Alfwyn criss-crossed his fingers and placed his hands on his lap. "Rhihalven are creatures who are very closely related to humans. A long time ago, we used to live in what is today called 'Europe.' Then, with the rise of the humans and their spread across Europe, we were driven to the icy northern lands.

Finally, we decided we could no longer live compatibly with the humans, who were very violent creatures and attacked our early tribes frequently. All we would do was protect ourselves."

"You should have scared them a little by making chairs appear!" Heath suggested. He grinned at the girls.

"They were not frightened of our magic because they knew Rhihalven by nature are peaceful creatures. We would refuse retaliation." Alfwyn leaned forward. "The attacks became so frequent that the Rhihalven formed a council and decided to build a homeland away from where the humans were living. We talked to other magical creatures who had also been forced into hiding to prevent attacks. We eventually convinced them to come with us."

"There are others?" Martina asked.

"Yes, many, many others." Alfwyn leaned back and rested his hands on the arms of the chair. "The ancient Rhihalven, who you might know as 'Neanderthals,' built a world under the human world. They began by tunneling underground just a little ways. Then, using a powerful space-bending spell and some other very intricate magic, they were able to create the world you see here, which folds in upon itself. If you were to actually see how much space this all takes up, you would be greatly impressed." Alfwyn lowered his voice. "I would say that all of Sheardland could fit in a human closet."

Alfwyn stood and approached the fish tank. Dipping into a container, he pulled out a liberal amount of Freshwater Dragon Mix and sprinkled it into the top of the tank. Instantly, a swarm of scaly little dragons flew through the water and began chasing down the food. They were sunset shades of yellow, orange, and red.

"Wow," Martina mouthed as she watched the dragons feeding. She so wanted to trust Alfwyn and believe his stories, but she was still nervous. What if he was lying about Mr. Willoughby being friends with these Rhihalven creatures? Mr. Willoughby had talked about Sheardland in his stories, but he only mentioned Fairies and Elves, creatures that they had heard of before.

"Like Sychateros chasing sweets." Alfwyn stared at the dragons feeding. "You can come look," he offered.

Martina, Heath, and London all jumped up and ran over to the tank. Multi-colored stones, a castle, and plants dotted the bottom of the tank. The dragons darted about in the water, feeding and chasing each other playfully.

"They sure are quick," London said.

The group watched the dragons tearing the food apart and swimming in the tank for a moment.

"Can you all perform magic?" Heath asked. "Like a magician?"

"Well, yes and no," Alfwyn answered. "We can all perform magic. However, our magic is nothing like a magician's hoax. I never have, for example, found it pertinent to saw any creature in half for entertainment of a crowd. Those are more tricks than magic."

"Why didn't the ancient Rhihalven just fight back," London asked, "instead of letting people attack them?"

"If we had fought back, do you think that you three would be sitting here right now?" Alfwyn said. "The Rhihalven could have made short work of all the humans without receiving so much as a scratch in return. We wanted to ensure that humans, as well as all the other species, could share this planet together."

"How did Mr. Willoughby know about the Rhihalven if no one else does?" Martina asked.

"Mr. Willoughby is a special case," Alfwyn answered. "Alas, it is getting late. Would you like to be our guests here at Adalborg tonight? The rooms are cozy, and the beds are the most comfortable on Earth or in Sheardland."

"But our parents might notice we are gone if we stay," Martina said.

"You have nothing to worry about," Alfwyn answered. "When any human travels to Sheardland, time on the Earth's surface stops. So no one will ever know you left."

"That makes sense, now," Heath said. "The clock only showed 5 minutes missing when we first went down the stairs. Remember, I said I thought we were gone longer."

A worried expression crossed London's face. "If we stay here very long, won't we age faster than everyone on Earth? Won't we look older? We could actually be sixteen, but the people on Earth will think we are old-looking thirteen-year-olds."

"We won't be able to get our licenses until we are nineteen," Heath said.

"That would be awful," Martina agreed.

"If you are worried about aging while you are here, have no fear," Alfwyn said. "Some of our top chemists have devised an elixir that will give you back the time you missed on Earth. It is a very effective de-aging solution: Dechronstructive Potion. No one will know the difference."

"You made a potion just for Mr. Willoughby?" Heath asked.

"Yes, we did," Alfwyn said, "but when we first worked with it, we gave Art way too high a strength. He decreased in age by several years every time we gave it to him. He did not even realize it himself until he was a good deal younger than he had been. He ended up living one hundred three years." Alfwyn laughed exhaustively. "That was so funny. He was fifty years old, and he was behaving like a teenager!"

Finally, Martina voiced her thoughts. "So why would he give me the music box with the clue about the entrance if no one is supposed to know about your world?"

"Awhile ago," Alfwyn began, "Mr. Willoughby and I agreed that if something should happen to him, we should have another ambassador from the humans to visit the Rhihalven. He insisted that it be up to his discretion. I trusted him. And here you are. *I knew there would be three of you*," he said mysteriously.

"Why three?" Heath queried.

"There are always three," Martina answered, shocking herself. She didn't know how she knew, but she knew that had to be correct.

"There are three of everything in all your Earthly books," Alfwyn said. "Three wishes, three dangerous tasks, three tries to get something right. I suspected Mr. Willoughby would do something so clever." Alfwyn winked at Martina. Growing serious, he walked toward the door. "You can decide by morning if you want to be the new ambassadors from the human realm. Mr. Willoughby was our honored guest here all the time. My family will not mind at all if you stay."

Martina looked toward the window. A short while ago, they had been marched through the town as the sun peeked at them over the distant hills. In the amount of time they had been in the Head Rhihalva's home, the sun had set, and replacing it were stars set on a jet black sky. Streetlights were turning on as she gazed out the window.

"I have one more question," Martina said. "Are we really underground? I got turned around when we came down the stairs."

"Indeed you are," Alfwyn responded. "Our weather Rhihalva takes care of the sun, moon, and stars. He is quite adept with it. The sun and moon are bewitched to travel across our sky like yours, but he handles the sunsets and the placement of the stars himself." Alfwyn gestured at the sky. "Oh, and the weather, of course. Just last night, we had a splendid sunset with lots of purple and green. It was lovely. A gifted painter, truly." Alfwyn mused on about the sunset.

"Purple and green?" Heath interjected. Without waiting for an answer, he turned to the girls and grinned. "That would be great."

Martina smiled, though her stomach was full of butterflies at the prospect of staying in this strange place. "What do you guys think? Should we stay?"

London nodded, her eyes sparkling with excitement. "I don't know if I can sleep, though. I'm so excited for tomorrow."

"Heath?"

Heath nodded assent to Martina.

She smiled at Alfwyn. "I think we'll all stay," she said bravely.

"Excellent, I need to make a few plans for tomorrow," Alfwyn said. "And you all need to get to bed." He motioned for them to wait there and disappeared through a door. Returning, he was accompanied by a round-bellied Rhihalva with extremely curly dark hair. His head and full beard were nothing compared to the large tufts bursting from his shirt collar and around his cuffs. The Rhihalva's black eyes were dull and tired, but he mustered up enough energy to scowl at the three humans.

"This is my assistant, Malandros," Alfwyn said. "He will take you to the guest tower." He bid them good night.

The three followed this lumbering Rhihalva, who led them from the office, up a spiraling stairway, and to the top of one of the towers. Martina frowned, wondering what they interrupted that made him so grouchy. The guy must really enjoy his work, especially to be at the office so late.

Malandros left them at the end of the hallway in the bedroom where they were to stay. He rested one hand on his over-sized belly and muttered something indistinguishable that conjured up bedroom furnishings and candles. Without another word to the group, he then retreated.

"Nice guy, huh?" London commented, wrinkling her nose. She wandered over to one of the beds and sat down.

The circular room was cozy in the dim light, with fluffy, brightly colored comforters and big piles of pillows on all three beds.

"Wow, this is really comfortable," Martina said as she fell backwards onto another bed and stared at the ceiling, realizing she felt utterly exhausted.

Heath tossed the book bag on a chair, collapsed on the third bed, and pretended to snore loudly.

As she looked up at the ceiling, Martina realized they hadn't prepared for spending the night here. She had no pajamas, no toothbrush, nothing at all. Nasty morning breath was not something she was looking forward to when they returned to speak to Alfwyn the next day.

Someone knocked on the door just then, and Martina bounded over to open it.

A tall Rhihalva with one long dark braid walked into the room without making a sound as she stepped. She looked young, except for the few strands of grey that tinged her beautiful glossy hair. She placed a pile of clothes on the dresser and approached the center of the room, her mauve gown swinging gently as she walked. "I am Parisa, Alfwyn's wife. I brought you each something to sleep in. I hope it is to your liking." She gestured to the pile on the dresser.

The trio walked over to see what she had brought. Lying there were three sets of clothes just like what all the other Rhihalven wore.

Martina picked up a long nightgown of a velvety cloth so light she barely felt it. Suspicious, she held the gown up to the light and discovered that you couldn't see through it. It was bubble-gum pink, not her favorite pink, but she didn't mind.

Parisa clapped her hands twice, and a screen appeared in a corner of the room for them to change behind. While they changed, Parisa said, "Breakfast is first thing in the morning. Showers are down the hall whenever you need them. Then comes the fun part: you get the grand tour of Sheardland!"

"I suppose it's settled," Martina thought. "We're going to continue Mr. Willoughby's work. I guess this is really what he meant in his note to London's dad." Although she was excited to find out about this magical world they had stumbled into, she was still apprehensive. She had read enough books— and certainly listened to Mr. Willoughby enough—to know that things might not be as they seem.

Sure, Fairies and Elves and such probably lived here, but dragons or giant scorpions or something else devious might be here, too. Maybe once she had been on the tour of Sheardland, she would somehow be able to spot the sinister part of the world before she got close enough to see any fanged beasties. Martina's stomach flip-flopped as she battled fear and excitement.

"It is such a beautiful place, as you will see," Parisa was saying. "You three will have a wonderful time. Oh, and you have not met my children yet. Tomorrow will be such a big day. Make sure you get plenty of rest."

"I don't think that will be a problem," Heath said. "I almost fell asleep as soon as I laid down."

"These are excellent beds," Parisa said, "made from giant woolly worm hair. We raise them and harvest their hair right here in Sheardland. I am certain the tour guide will take you there tomorrow."

"Can you ride the giant woolly worms?" Heath sprouted a goofy grin as he pretended to lasso the dresser.

"No." Parisa chuckled. "They are only raised for their hair. But, you may run into something you can ride tomorrow. We were able to rescue many of the magical creatures from the surface so they would not be abused or hunted to extinction."

Parisa tucked them into bed, which was odd because their parents had long ago stopped that. "Did my husband bring you here, or is he still in the office at this late hour?"

"I think he's still in the office," Martina said. "He said he had arrangements to make, so he sent Malandros with us."

"It is strange that Malandros is working so late tonight," Parisa commented. "He is pretty quiet, though. He tends to keep to himself."

"It's like he has something to hide!" Heath blurted out, acting like he was hiding behind his hands.

Martina and London both chuckled.

Parisa laughed. "It is best to work with someone who is quiet than someone who will talk all day. That is one reason Alfwyn chose Malandros. I suppose they are finishing up a project late. That happens sometimes when you are Head Rhihalva." She approached the door. "You should get some sleep." She uttered "delumen," and the light grew so low that only outlines and shadows could be seen. "Sleep well. Visit pleasant places in your dreams." Parisa exited the room.

Naturally, as soon as she was gone, the three sat up in bed and began chattering excitedly.

"Tomorrow is going to be so great," London exclaimed. "I wonder what we'll get to see."

"Are you guys sure you want to do this?" Martina said. "I mean, we don't really know what's down here. Maybe we should look for the notes that Alfwyn thought Mr. Willoughby had left us."

"Remember how I told you there was a treasure behind the ice cream machine?" Heath began. "And that we had to turn the handles? So let's just say you should start trusting my instincts." He puffed up his chest. "We'll be fine."

"You don't know that," Martina said. "But as long as you guys think it's safe to stay, then I guess we can."

"You worry too much," Heath said. "Where's your sense of adventure? We need to get out and explore the world before we're so old that we have to worry about taxes and car payments and all that other stuff that my mom's always talking to Cerberus about."

"Who's Cerberus?" London asked.

"It's the three-headed dog from Greek myth that guards the gates to Hades." Martina chuckled. "But I think Heath's referring to his three sisters."

"Right-o," Heath answered.

Eventually, they grew silent and were soon sleeping soundly on their giant woolly-worm-hair mattresses.

     *   *   *   *   *   *

Shiny yellow eyes stared vacantly out from the darkness under the dresser at the end of the room. The creature's breathing halted momentarily when it spotted what it had been looking for. Quietly, the creature retreated. It had to tell the others. What they most desired had practically been delivered right into their pockets.

Chapter 6 – No Tears for What Spilt

The next morning, they were awakened by a crash and the sounds of a scuffle.

Martina sat up in bed, pulling the covers up to her armpits.

Heath jumped out of his bed and looked suspiciously at the mattress.

London screamed and snatched one of her shoes, ready to whack something with it.

Martina spotted the contents of the book bag strewn all over the floor. It was the only thing that seemed unusual about the room. Now, there was total silence.

"I *think* there's *something* in my mattress." He grabbed a water bottle from the floor and wielded it, ready to strike.

Martina climbed out of bed and approached Heath's mattress as well, but London remained in the safety of her bed.

As Martina approached Heath's bed and reached for the covers, a sneeze echoed from under the dresser. She cautiously picked up a flashlight and dragged Heath slowly toward the dresser for backup.

Martina flicked on the flashlight and crouched, prepared for something crawly and disgusting to come running out from under the dresser.

As Martina shined the flashlight around in the darkness, Heath held the water bottle ready.

When Martina saw what was hiding there, she was completely surprised.

"Come here, little guy," Heath cooed gently.

London jumped out of her bed. "What is it? A puppy? I love puppies!" She landed on her knees by the dresser. When she looked, she leapt back and wrinkled up her nose. "What is that?"

Heath, too, peeked under the dresser. "He and his buddies are thinking the same thing about us." He pointed at the far dark corner.

"Stay right there while we get Alfwyn," Martina said to the creatures. "I promise we won't hurt you."

"She lies," Heath whispered.

Martina gave Heath a sour look as she headed for the door.

Before she could turn the knob, though, the creatures crawled out from under the dresser. There were five of them, each a chubby little man no more than eight inches tall sporting grizzly beards, boots, and hats. Their eyes, now a bright green in the natural light, were wide with fear. The largest one was carrying a sock with a blue toe.

"That's my sock, buddy." Heath yanked the sock out of his tiny hands and put it on.

Then, someone knocked on the door.

Martina opened it and found both Alfwyn and Parisa standing there.

"I'm so glad you're here," Martina exclaimed. "They broke into our room."

The pair at the door stared at the little men in the middle of the room. "What are you doing in here?" Parisa scolded. "You have frightened our guests."

"Didn't I say yesterday that under no circumstances were they to be bothered with your silliness?" Alfwyn said to them. "I know you have their socks. Give them back now." He waited for them to dig through their packs. Finally, they had each produced another one of the socks, bringing the total up to six.

"Were you guys fighting over my sock?" Heath asked.

Martina laughed as she realized what Heath was talking about. The odd number of little men with the even number of socks was probably the source of the ruckus that woke everyone that morning.

"This sort of scuffling reminds me of the legend of the Sycateros." Parisa looked disappointed as she said it.

Finally, one spoke to defend his comrades. "We are researchers for the great Sock Gnome Nation." The Sock Gnome spoke eagerly in a high, but dignified nasally voice. "We were commanded to bring your socks back to our leader so we can learn about your strange species. Once we examine them, we would bring them back to you." The Sock Gnomes waited, eyes open wide with the appearance of innocence.

Martina was not convinced by this speech.

"The Sock Gnomes are not supposed to leave Sheardland, and they do not return the socks they take," Alfwyn said. He turned to the Gnomes. "You have them stockpiled *somewhere*. When are you going to understand that you cannot learn much about their species from their socks?"

The Sock Gnomes appeared offended by Alfwyn's accusations and whispered in angry hisses.

"You can return to the Sock Gnome Nation if I have your word that you will not sneak in here anymore to steal our visitors' socks," Alfwyn said.

The Sock Gnomes agreed, bowed, and then scuttled off to a corner of the room where a heating duct had been left open. All five of them disappeared through the hole, pulling the vent shut after they were gone.

Martina wasn't sure what to think. After only one night in Sheardland, they had already met several creatures she wasn't sure she could trust.

"Why don't you dress so we can head down to breakfast?" Parisa said after the Gnomes left.

A short time later, the three of them, Alfwyn, and Parisa were eating in Adalborg's dining room. After some time, the couple's own children paraded in, the ten-year-old triplets, Haldor, Torvald, and Brantrod, with the baby Ilona.

The Rhihalven children were smartly dressed, the boys in tunics and pants and the baby in a tot-sized dress of emerald green. Hair was neatly combed, and a smile was on every face. They boys chattered excitedly about the upcoming school day as they approached the table.

"That's a little different from human children," Martina thought. How many times had she been dragged out of bed and slouched her way to breakfast while grouching about going to school? Then she remembered her manners. "Good morning!"

She was greeted the same way by the triplets. Ilona burbled something cute that made Martina smile.

Parisa scooped Ilona up and placed her at the table. She pointed at the clock, which was scrolling through the list of items to be done that day, closer and closer to the time for the tour to begin. "We should hurry," she said. "There is not much time left to get ready."

Alfwyn soon whisked off toward his office.

After the triplets had eaten, they ran out the door to go to school.

Martina, Heath, and London devoured their food: delicious fire oat muffins and baked copy cattle with fresh Rhihalvaberries. Martina was skeptical at first but soon discovered that everything reminded her of something she had eaten back home. She was surprised to discover, however, that copy cattle was one unusual meat that didn't taste a thing like chicken.

*   *   *   *   *   *

After they were ready for the day, Martina, Heath, and London headed for the front door to wait with Parisa for the tour guide, who was supposed to pick them up at the house.

Parisa paused to grab a bag of what appeared to be sawdust from the cupboard in the front hall.

"What is that stuff?" Heath asked.

Parisa sprinkled it on an ant hill in the front yard as she muttered something unintelligible. "This rids the yard of ants," Parisa answered. "Though we prefer to live in harmony with them, they will insist on making mountains on our lawn. It just is not safe for Ilona and the boys."

"I wonder if that stuff works on other types of unwanted guests," Heath said to Martina.

The evil glint in Heath's eye told her that he was thinking about his sisters. "So you want your mom's attention all the time, then?" Martina laughed.

"Good point." Heath sighed loudly.

As they waited for the tour, Martina asked Parisa, "I was wondering if Mr. Willoughby got my music box in Sheardland. Do you know where it's from?"

Parisa smiled at her. "That music box of yours was a project I worked on. It was a special order by several of our researchers in Human Affairs, and it was made specifically for Art. They wanted to present his with an unusual gift to thank him for everything he had done for them. He greatly advanced their research because of the knowledge he provided them. He used to report important events from the human realm to them at weekly meetings." Parisa paused as Ilona struggled to get down.

"So Mr. Willoughby's important work was to tell the Rhihalven about everything that happens on the surface?" Heath asked. "Cool. He was like a reporter."

"Not exactly," Parisa said. "That was something else he did because he knew the Rhihalven were as curious about humans as he was about them. The important part of his work was a little more involved. For instance, he discovered—"

Suddenly, a creature the size of a small dog raced around the corner of the building and smacked into London, nearly knocking her over.

"Come here, Pyra," Parisa cooed. The lemony yellow creature ignored her prey and trotted over to her. A row of seafoam green plates protruded from its back. "This is our snapdragon, Pyra."

"Ooooh, a dragon," London said. "Can she breathe fire?"

"Not anymore," Parisa said. "We got her from a breeder, so she's been deflamed. But wild snapdragons can still breathe fire, so if you are out of Rhihalvberg, you should be careful of running into packs of them. They will torch you so fast you will not realize it until you are a charred pile of ashes. Is that not right, Pyra?" She fondly scratched the snapdragon behind her ears.

"Lovely," Martina thought. "Cute little dangerous pets lurking in the woods. Fun, fun."

Just then, a round, shiny vehicle that looked as though it were made of green glass pulled up in front of the building. Big black lettering on the side announced it as the "Lollie Trolley." It resembled trolleys from the surface, but it was floating above the ground and had no wheels. And obviously, trolleys aren't usually round.

Heath nudged Martina. "It's a UFO!"

"Ha. Ha," Martina said, wryly.

The few passengers on the Lollie Trolley seemed annoyed with the wait as a petite Rhihalva woman jumped from the driver's seat to greet the new guests. As she approached the group at Adalborg, the woman passed near the snapdragon, which emitted a snapping sound and turned itself into a flowering plant to hide.

"They are little cowards," Parisa said. She laughed at the snapdragon. "They think that transforming will hide them from anything they are afraid of, silly creatures." Parisa approached the tour guide and held her palm up to greet her with the magical ripples of light, the same way Alfwyn and Siofra had said "hello." "Hello, Chavdra. I am glad to see that you are giving the tour today."

Chavdra smiled in response. The petite Rhihalva looked young, especially with her short blond hair in braided pigtails. Her sleeveless red gown was tied at the waist with a black cord covered in gold stars, each reading "One Year of Outstanding Service." As she approached, Chavdra reached into the small black messenger bag she wore and pulled out tags for each of them.

Reaching the porch, she finally spoke in a high, boisterous voice that Martina found to be annoyingly sweet. "My name is Chavdra! I will be your tour guide for today. Please tell me your names and get on the bus, and we will be on our way." She leaned toward each human to get their names. Pointing at the name tags, she bewitched each one to read the name. Then, she affixed the tags to their clothes by saying, "Adhese." She spun around and started back to the trolley. "Follow me!"

Martina, Heath, and London waved at Parisa and climbed aboard. They quickly looked for a seat as the trolley wobbled a bit before it floated down the street. As they sat down, they were overcome with the scent of sour apple candy.

Martina was relieved to discover that the inside of the trolley remained stationary while the outside spun like a top, ferrying them off on their tour.

Heath leaned his face toward the seat in front of him and sniffed. Then, he grinned and licked the seat.

"Aw, you're disgusting, Heath," Martina said. She received dirty looks from the motley group of other passengers. Together, only about ten passengers made up the party. Aside from the tour guide, none of them appeared to be Rhihalven.

The trio could see the whole lot of their companions in the circular trolley. There were small creatures with huge butterfly wings, bluish-black hair, and pointed ears who remained stiffly facing forward. Others were misshapen beings that somewhat resembled pigs, like the ones Martina had first spotted having tea at Adalborg.

"Welcome to Lollie Trolley Tours!" Chavdra said. "We will be traveling all over Sheardland today. I hope everyone is ready for some fun and excitement."

"Woohoo!" Heath called.

"Shhhhh!" Martina hissed.

"I'm excited because the trolley is made of candy," Heath said.

"Oh, no," Chavdra began, "this trolley is one of the most up-to-date trolleys we have. It is made entirely out of a secret compound developed by the researchers at Human Affairs. They claim that humans actually eat the stuff this trolley is made of. Further studies have led our researchers to discover that this compound also makes a wonderful fuel. And who wants to eat something strong enough to propel a vehicle?" Chavdra paused as she went around a bend. Verdant hills took the place of the houses and the busy street they had just passed through.

"I'll eat almost anything," Heath muttered as he mock-lunged at Martina's arm.

"Maybe we should let Chavdra know that licking the seat turned you into a werewolf," London commented.

"To the left of the trolley, you can see Odhárna Fields and one of the fields where copy cattle are raised. They produce wonderful milk in several flavors. But copy cattle are difficult to work with sometimes. They are known for their ability to change into any creature that they may be looking in the eye. It must be awfully hard to milk something when its udders keep disappearing." Chavdra paused to allow the raucous laughter to die down.

"To the right, you will see the giant woolly worm ranch. I will park so we can get out and pet some of these lovely creatures." Chavdra stopped the trolley in the middle of the field. "Do watch your step please," she called.

The trio walked toward a black and brown striped woolly worm that was grazing on tree branches nearby. London grabbed Heath's arm just in time to keep him from stepping in a pile of worm dung the size of a shoebox.

"Whoa, that was close!" Heath said. "I would have sunk into that one up to my ankle. Nasty!"

Martina walked up to the very tame woolly worm and began stroking its hair.

"Humans have a legend about the woolly worm," Chavdra said. "They have a miniature species that is only inches long. It is said that when a person sees a woolly worm that is dark, the winter will be very harsh. If the woolly worm is light, then the winter will be very mild."

Martina nodded agreement when Chavdra glanced her way.

"However," Chavdra continued, "woolly worms are not really indicators of the weather. They like to eat leaves and grasses, and their hair can be harvested and used to make clothing and mattress stuffing." Soon, Chavdra led the group back to the trolley.

"I don't remember hearing stories about woolly worms forecasting the weather," London commented.

"My mom mentioned something about that once," Heath said. "I think she's crazy though."

Martina shushed them in case the other passengers realized they were humans who believed that stuff and who ate lollipops rather than riding around in them.

After stopping for the wooly worms, the trolley visited several other places in Sheardland. They saw Elfin Nook, Sock Gnome Nation, Fairy Grove, and several other sections as the trolley spun instantly through the long distances between each of the countries.

"This place really is perfect," Martina thought. "Everyone gets along. They visit each other's lands. It is so cool." She wondered, though, what exactly was Mr. Willoughby's important work? What was it that he discovered here?

During the final loop through Fairy Grove, after dropping off most of the other passengers at the main trolley station, Chavdra guided the trolley along a scenic route back to Rhihalvberg. She maneuvered them through a rough patch that led to a huge marshy area completely covered in dense trees with hanging mosses and vines clinging to them.

Martina exchanged confused looks with Heath and London as she heard crying coming from somewhere deep within its recesses. "Chavdra, does someone live in there," Martina said.

"Here, no," Chavdra said. "But let us make an impromptu stop. I just love impromptu stops." Chavdra screeched the trolley to a halt and leapt from the driver's seat. "Be careful. The ground is a bit unstable." Her squeaky voice squealed like the trolley's breaks.

The rest of the passengers filed out.

"What is this going to be?" Martina thought.

"This is the Swamp of Sorrows," Chavdra said. "Sort of a dreary place, is it not? I have never gone in here myself, never having a bad day in my life. But, this is the site to whence all sorrows have been banished."

"Sorrow, I hereby banish you from the kingdom," Heath said. "Go live in the swamp." Heath gestured with an imaginary sword at Martina.

The girls chuckled.

Chavdra continued her tale. "The first Head Rhihalva in Sheardland decreed that Rhihalvberg would be free from all sadness. He made it law that any upset Rhihalva was to come immediately to the Swamp of Sorrows."

"We all would have come here when Mr. Willoughby died," Martina thought.

"Then," Chavdra said, "the Rhihalva could enter the swamp and be purged of all sorrows by crying. Once the sorrow was gone, she would emerge happy again. Is that not wonderful? That is why the ground is soggy, from all the tears of poor, forlorn Rhihalven."

"Somehow, I don't think crying in the swamp would make me feel any better," London said.

"It is said that just entering the safety of these trees starts the healing process," Chavdra told them. "Sometimes, you can hear the sadness as bubbles pop and then are swallowed to the bottom again, just as you heard a few minutes ago. One can recall sorrows of the past by entering the swamp and requesting them."

Martina peered into the dense canopy to see if any bubbles were popping. "I wonder if Mr. Willoughby ever came here."

"That looks interesting," Heath said. "I know it's morbid, but I want to go see!"

"No way," London replied. "I would never go in there." She eyed the grimy oozing surface at the edge of the swamp.

"I bet they have loads of cool bugs in there," Heath said in his awful Australian accent. "Maybe even some fish that will gnaw off your legs!" Heath rubbed his hands together.

"Hurry! Back on the trolley," Chavdra said. "I thought of one other place that may be of interest to you humans." Chavdra trotted past them and hopped back into the driver's seat.

As soon as everyone had boarded the trolley again, Chavdra floored the pedal. In a few minutes, she dropped off the rest of the passengers at the trolley stop, leaving only Martina, Heath, and London on the tour.

When she was almost back to Rhihalvberg, Chavdra turned the trolley abruptly and headed into a pass between the two mountains at the far west of town. A tangle of flowering trees and bushes obscured their view and nearly blocked the path. She stopped the Lollie Trolley just before they arrived at the thick vegetation. "We will have to walk from here. Follow me please," she said to them.

The plants thinned as the group walked until they finally emerged into an open valley of wildflowers. Between the field of flowers and the far mountain, rose a vast orchard. Thousands of trees stood in perfect rows, each bearing fruits that looked like they had been dipped in sparkling sugars.

Trickling down the farthest mountain was a waterfall that ended in a stream winding its way through the back of the valley. They stared in awe at the beauty of this hidden garden.

Gesturing behind her, Chavdra announced, "This is the Garden of Afalonga. Through the fruits on the trees, one can achieve a sort of immortality. Each fruit contains a dream that has been or will be dreamed. They are not consumed by being eaten, but by being dreamed."

"I wonder what kind of dreams ugli fruit or horned melon would give you," Heath mused.

"That sounds disturbing," Martina said.

"As a Rhihalva has a dream," Chavdra continued, "the particular fruit that provided the dream crystallizes so the dream is safe within its protective skin. We call these trees Dreaming Trees. They are the reason why Rhihalven always have wonderful dreams."

"Do you never have nightmares?" Martina queried.

"I am not sure what that is." Chavdra smiled. "All our dreams are pleasant, if that is what you are asking."

"Look. Little Rhihalva kids." Heath pointed at the little ones flitting between the trees.

"Those are nymphs, and they are actually adults," Chavdra said. "They live in the garden and tend to the dreaming trees."

In the distance, the willowy nymphs did look like children running and playing among the trees. Their gossamer clothes floated gently in the light breeze as they climbed up and down from their tree houses.

"I'm getting hungry looking at all that fruit," London said.

"Rightfully so," Chavdra said. "It is nearly time for everyone to eat. We must hurry back to Adalborg." Again, Chavdra flew past them and hopped back into her chair. She started the trolley and waited for them to climb onto the benches. Once everyone was seated again, she turned the trolley back toward Rhihalvberg.

As they approached the first building at the edge of town, Chavdra slowed the trolley. "Would you like to see where Parisa works? It will only take a minute. You have already seen Alfwyn's office, and Parisa's workplace is open to the public."

"Sure," Martina answered. "If it's not too far out of the way."

"It is right in front of you," Chavdra said. She parked the trolley beside the three-story building, which bore a huge red and white sign announcing "Marvin's Magical Toys."

As they entered, they were greeted by a Rhihalva woman at the front desk. "Hello, Chavdra. Good to see you." She returned to the purchase she was ringing up.

"What a fascinating place," Martina said.

The inside was open to the ceiling, which was swirling with a colorful exhibition like looking through a kaleidoscope. Row upon row of books, games, and toys lined the show floor. A long metal stairway led up to the second level balcony, which encircled the entire level. And a hallway at the back of the store led to the offices of the designers and builders.

Ecstatic Rhihalva children scampered about, picking up dolls that fly and invisible toy puppies that bark and pull their leashes, among the many other fascinating finds.

"Parisa has a pretty cool job if she gets to come in here every day," Heath said.

"Yeah, I don't think I'd complain about staying late at the office ever," London said.

"I knew you would like it," Chavdra said. "Now, let us head back to Adalborg before I make you too late to eat with the family."

A short time later, while eating dinner, Martina, Heath, and London discussed the trip they had taken.

"I really wish we had visited the weather Rhihalva," Martina said. "That would have been great. I wanted to see him painting his sunsets."

"No one really goes to his lab," Alfwyn said. "He likes to keep to himself."

"You know, I've been wondering how Great-Granddad found Sheardland," London said.

"Around the time the ice cream shop was being built," Alfwyn began, "the Rhihalven were building more exits into the world above. Always sneaking to the surface, the Sock Gnomes told Redmund, the Head Rhihalva at the time, about ice cream, and he wanted to taste it. He could not resist the temptation, and drew the plans to extend an exit into the shop." Leaning forward in his chair, Alfwyn continued.

"Once the exit was built, Redmund waited for word from the Sock Gnomes about the right time to use it. One night, soon after the completion, a breech was noted at exit number 248 (the one in the ice cream shop). Mr. Willoughby had been cleaning the machine and turned all three knobs to the left. Of course, you know that causes the door to open."

"Ah, memories," Heath said.

Alfwyn chuckled. "So Mr. Willoughby wandered down the stairs and into the travel office. When he did, complete pandemonium broke out. At first, the Alvar wanted to execute him. However, their captain insisted that the Head Rhihalva see the result of his mistake. There had been a bit of a disagreement between the Elves and the Rhihalven at the time and—"

"So the Alvar are Elves?" Heath interrupted.

"Yes, an Elf Army. Elves are great warriors and have very little magic anymore. The Alvar guard all Sheardland's exits," Alfwyn cleared his throat. "So the captain brought Art to Redmund, and Redmund was delighted. He had never met a human before, because of the strict laws we have about visiting the human realm. Redmund kept Art here and tested him to see how he would react to knowing that the Rhihalven had magical powers. As it turns out, Art was just as fascinated with us as Redmund was with him."

"That's so cool," Martina said.

Alfwyn continued. "They became good friends, and Art began to visit often. And luckily, he never had to hide where he was going because whenever he would enter into our world, time would stop on Earth."

"Speaking of time standing still, tonight we have a special treat for you all," Parisa said. "One of the toymakers I design for is the great puppet-master Arist Thanatolaus. At our theater, he will be putting on a show for all the Rhihalven using some new puppets I have designed. Maybe we can introduce you to some Rhihalven who worked with Art on his projects."

"What sort of projects did Mr. Willoughby do? And what did he discover?" Martina asked. Unfortunately, her questions were lost among everyone else's excitement, especially that of the triplets.

"Puppet shows are fun. It is the best entertainment ever." Haldor exclaimed.

"Yeah, we get to see one almost every week. We always look forward to it," Torvald echoed his brother's enthusiasm.

"It is the highlight of my week," Brantrod said. "They are so exciting." He grinned at his brothers.

"Are there musicians?" Heath asked eagerly.

"Are they magical puppets?" London asked.

"Alas, but we do not use musicians at our puppet shows," Alfwyn laughed. "And, yes, they are magical puppets. Our puppeteers perform the play much as actors do, behind the stage, and the puppets mimic their actions. I am sure you will find it fascinating. "

*   *   *   *   *   *

Two hours later, Martina, Heath, and London found themselves seated in an outdoor theater bored out of their minds. Although the show had already been going on for twenty minutes, nothing exciting had happened. The novelty of bewitched puppets had worn off in the first five minutes. For the next fifteen, they had stared at the stage much like they stared at some of their teachers.

Martina thought it was strange that the Rhihalven went to such lengths to protect themselves from conflict and sadness. It seemed that the Rhihalven hadn't dealt with anything bad other than what happened in the carvings on the door to Adalborg. Maybe that's why they had nothing exciting to portray in their puppet shows. All that happened was common, everyday life enacted by puppets that bobbed across the stage free of attachments to their puppeteers. Their dreams came prepackaged from trees, they got along with all the other countries, and their entertainment didn't have a twist or an argument. What were they hiding?

"How are they doing this?" Heath whispered to Martina. He gestured toward the Branimirs. All of them, even baby Ilona, were hypnotized by the sight of the cloth actors. The entire audience stared raptly at the stage in total silence.

"My guess is that they don't know what they are missing, so they think this is great entertainment," Martina said. She kept an eye out to be sure she wasn't disturbing any of the Rhihalven.

Suddenly, London grabbed Martina's sleeve and pointed across the theater to a man who was standing up in the last row. "Isn't that Malandros, the guy who showed us to our room last night?" she asked, just as the man ducked through the exit.

Martina turned in time to miss him.

"I guess he's bored, too," Heath said too loudly.

Martina and London shot him looks of death as audience members around them shushed them.

"Maybe he's going to the bathroom," Martina said, certain that only they were pained by this performance.

For another thirty minutes, the puppets dazzled the audience and were greeted with a chorus of "ooohs" and "ahhhs" from the Rhihalven surrounding Martina, Heath, and London.

"When will this be over?" Heath moaned in Martina's ear.

Martina ignored him, annoyed by his persistent rudeness toward the Rhihalven. Sure, they were weird, but she didn't want to make them mad.

Finally, the word "Intermission" flashed on the curtain at the back of the stage, and the puppets froze in place. The entire audience rose and headed toward the concessions.

As they stretched by their seats, London turned to Martina and Heath. Leaning in close to them, she whispered, "He never came back."

"Who never came back?" Heath asked.

"Not so loud! Do you mean Malandros?" Martina whispered.

"Yeah, I got so bored that I kept an eye out for him," London said. "But he never went back to his seat."

The Branimir boys wanted to get some Insect Bites, so Martina, Heath, and London followed the family to the concession stands. Alfwyn bought Insect Bites for everyone since the humans had never tried them before.

The first thing that surprised Martina was that he paid with what appeared to be golden kidney beans. The second thing that surprised her was that what she held in her hand looked and moved exactly like a real insect.

The triplets poured a handful out of the bag and popped them into their mouths. As they chewed, London looked like she might get sick.

"Just try them," Haldor coaxed. "They are not real bugs."

Heath tossed his into his mouth first and grinned. "These are good."

Martina threw hers into her mouth before she could think about it. As it moved on her tongue, she found it hard to get the courage up to bite down. Soon, the hair on the bug's back melted like cotton candy. Finally, unable to handle the furry bug tickling the inside of her mouth any more, she chomped down, and nearly spit the thing on the ground. When she realized that what was trickling out was not bug blood, but caramel, she began chewing on it just as the others were. And she found herself wanting to try another.

As she reached into the bag, a bell chimed, signaling five minutes left of intermission. Across the hallway, Martina spotted Malandros chatting pleasantly with a Rhihalva wearing a long black cape over a golden yellow tunic. The Rhihalva had an overall crispness that contrasted with Malandros's frizzy hair, large belly, and slumped posture, making them look like an unlikely pair. This Rhihalva's neatly trimmed and parted hair, his sparkling dark brown eyes, and his rugged good looks made him a prominent character in the room. As he spoke, Malandros showed a mouth full of crooked, squarish teeth that couldn't compare to his companion's perfectly straight ones.

Suddenly, the well-kept man pivoted gracefully on his heel and swaggered toward where the Branimirs were gathered.

"Arist, the show has been wonderful this evening," Parisa commented.

"Ah, all because of your lovely designs, Lady Branimir," he responded with an oily tone. He bowed respectfully to Parisa and Alfwyn and then announced that he must be going.

"We should be heading back to our seats, as well, if we want to catch the beginning of the second act." Alfwyn ushered his children back toward the theater.

"Yes, we wouldn't want to miss that, eh?" Heath poked Martina in the ribs with his elbow.

She swatted him away and walked on. Her shoes made sticky noises, though. "Ew! What's this stuff all over the floor?" Martina stopped and stared at the shimmery yellow substance that had been tracked by numerous pairs of shoes.

"Looks like butter, doesn't it?" London replied.

"I bet someone spilled their popcorn," Heath said. "Who knows what they put in that butter? I shouldn't let all this good butter go to waste."

"But butter isn't sticky. It feels like soda," Martina said.

Heath shrugged and leaned over, acting like he would run his finger through the stuff.

Martina shook her head, but London immediately said, "Don't eat that. Ew!" She grabbed his tunic to keep him from leaning over.

Heath laughed and gave her a light shove.

Martina ignored their banter and returned to her seat, vaguely pondering why sticky yellow soda would be on the floor when she hadn't seen soda of any color since they arrived in Sheardland.

Another hour passed with as much excitement as the first hour of the show. After the final act, the Rhihalven clapped and cheered for Arist as he bowed with his puppets. Then finally, they were able to go home.

That night, Martina stayed awake a long time thinking about what she had seen that day. They visited so many different places and people. None of this seemed real to her. She rolled over and tried to shut out the day and relax.

"I have to find out what Mr. Willoughby was up to down here and what he discovered," she thought. "And why do the Rhihalven avoid anything that might upset them? They aren't even allowed to dream."

This got her thinking about what her world was like right now. On the surface of the Earth, everyone must be frozen in position, doing whatever they were doing when she had entered the ice cream machine. She hoped her family was ok.

As she was just about to fall asleep, a scream shattered the night. All three of them sat up and jumped out of bed.

"What was that?" London said.

They all huddled together, waiting for the screaming to cease.

It was only their second night in a magical land, and they had been awakened by strange noises both nights. Martina wondered if they should run because they were in danger or if they were safer where they were. Just after the screaming stopped, the door burst open, answering her question.

Chapter 7 – Dreams that Shatter the Night

Without knocking, Parisa ran into the room. "You have to come quickly. It is so terrible. Nobody is safe." She grabbed their arms and dragged all three of them with her down the stairs. She led them down a corridor which took them to another one of the towers. In this tower, the family's bedrooms were all side by side. Upon entering the triplet's room, they found Alfwyn sitting with his children, hugging them and trying to calm them down. Sweat trickled down his forehead as he told them not to worry.

"What happened?" Martina asked.

Everyone began talking at once. They were so distraught that Martina couldn't make out any of it. Parisa shook her head and put her hands over her face. Wiping away tears, she began explaining what was going on when everyone grew silent.

"I thought I was sleeping, but horrible things kept happening," she said. "I know I was not dreaming. Dreams are pleasant. I awoke sweating, and Alfwyn had the same experience. Ilona was crying, and the boys were screaming. I grabbed Ilona and brought her in here with the boys. They said the same thing happened to them." Turning to her family, huddled on the bed, she embraced them and cried.

Alfwyn spoke up. "It is as if our minds are being controlled by something bad. All our good dreams disappeared."

"Are they having nightmares?" Martina whispered to Heath and London.

"There's only one way to find out," Heath said. "Were you able to scream or run when all the bad things were happening to you?" he asked the Branimirs.

"No, it was just awful," Brantrod said.

"I tried to scream for help," Haldor said.

"I tried to run away, but I could not move," Torvald said.

"I could not say anything," Haldor added.

Ilona was still crying hysterically while Parisa rocked her gently, patting her back.

Martina frowned. What had happened was so obvious to her. Could it really be that simple? She thought that maybe telling them what she thought would help to calm their fears. "I think you all were just having nightmares," she said.

They stopped crying and stared at her. "What's a nightmare?" Torvald asked.

"It's like a dream, but it's not fun or good," Heath replied. "Everything that happens is scary."

"It's like having a dream about your worst fears," London added. "So you wake up scared. Then you go back to sleep, and you're fine."

"There's nothing to worry about," Martina said. "I've had lots of nightmares. They can't hurt you. It really is *just* a bad dream."

"Did you all just have nightmares, too?" Alfwyn seemed to ponder their calmness.

"I didn't," Martina replied. The others shook their heads.

"So, why did we have nightmares?" Parisa asked nervously.

"That is strange that *all* of you had nightmares at the same time," London said.

"Maybe something has been bothering everyone," Martina said. "Has there been a problem here that you're concerned about?"

"But the baby had nightmares, too," Heath said.

"I don't know then. It's just a coincidence, maybe," Martina said.

"I don't think so. Look." London pointed out the window.

Rhihalven were running into the streets shrieking, as if their world was coming to an end. Not one of them had ever experienced a nightmare before.

Martina wanted to laugh, but tried to place herself in the shoes of those who had no idea what was going on. They probably believed the nightmare was reality or a foreboding prediction of what was to come. It was as if Martina were a child again. She knew the fear.

By then, the family finally seemed to calm down.

"They need me to help them understand," Alfwyn said. "I must explain what has happened."

Alfwyn headed for the window and opened it. Touching his throat and uttering a voice-amplifying charm, "Deisopia," he addressed the Rhihalven. "Please go back in your houses. You are merely experiencing bad dreams. You have nothing to fear. I will do my best to figure out what is wrong." The streets cleared as everyone sheepishly returned to their homes.

*   *   *   *   *   *

Throughout that night and the next two, Martina, Heath, and London didn't get much sleep with all the screaming and crying echoing through the house. The entire family was having nightmares every time they tried to sleep. Throughout the day, as everyone tried to carry on as usual, they found it difficult not to fall asleep when they sat down. Finally, on the third night, Martina sat up in her bed, worried that this would go on forever, and anxious to return home if it didn't stop soon.

"This is hopeless," she said into the darkness. She could just make out the shapes of Heath and London as they, too, sat up in their beds. "This has never happened to me before. If I have a nightmare, I just calm down, go back to sleep, and don't have any more."

"Maybe they can't calm themselves down," London said.

"Yeah, these are their first nightmares," Heath added.

"But no one does this. It's just not normal," Martina reminded them. "Without sleep, no one will be able to function normally at all. They are already so sleep-deprived that they're like zombies."

"This is how the world is going to end," Heath said. "Zombie apocalypse of Sheardland. That would be an awesome movie."

The girls laughed tiredly.

"I don't see how they have never had any nightmares and then constantly have them for three nights in a row," London said.

"Maybe I should have brought my tuba," Heath said. "That would have chased their nightmares away." He smiled, apparently satisfied at the thought of his mass concert.

"Something has to be wrong in the Garden of Afalonga," Martina said. "They have never had nightmares because of it, right?"

"The what?" Heath asked.

"That was that place with the dreaming trees, right?" London asked.

Martina nodded. "Maybe the trees didn't get watered enough. Something must be wrong there for it to go on this long."

London's face lit up. "So, all the Rhihalven have to do is find out what's up with the trees."

"Or we can," Martina said.

"Are you nuts?" London said. "We don't even know if we are allowed in there alone. And if we were, what could we do?"

"And, not to damper your enthusiasm for doing things we shouldn't be doing," Heath grinned, "but shouldn't we just tell Alfwyn and let him take care of it?"

"Are you kidding? Not one of the Rhihalven is in any sort of shape to handle this," Martina said.

"They're so exhausted they'd probably fall asleep halfway there." She tried to suppress the thought that they still hadn't found out what it was that Mr. Willoughby had discovered in Sheardland. Hopefully, it wasn't something that came out at night.

"So, when should we go?" Heath asked.

"Let's start now," Martina said. "If we can figure out why the Rhihalven are having bad dreams, then we can help them—and us—get some sleep." She climbed out of bed and struggled into the gown she had worn that day. "We have to make sure we're quiet, though. I don't want someone getting cranky and telling us we can't go."

The trio tip-toed down the stairs. As they approached the front door, they found Pyra stretched out on her back sleeping soundly on the rug. Quietly, they slipped past her and out the door. They crept down the street, past houses where an occasional light was on. Faint screams could be heard from a nightmare victim's room. Because the street lights were lit, they had no trouble seeing where they were going until they reached the edge of town.

Martina paused as her eyes adjusted to the dark. In the silence of the night, she heard a click nearby just as light flooded the ground at her feet. Looking up, she saw Heath grinning and wielding a flashlight.

"Thought we might need this," he said.

Martina was relieved that Heath had, once again, come prepared.

Following the road out of town, the trio crossed the bridge and headed toward the mountains to the west, taking the same route the Lolley Trolley had taken to bring them back from the Garden.

"I'm glad there aren't any turns to remember," Martina said, "and that the mountains are so easy to spot."

"That should make it easier to find the Garden," London said.

Further from town, the screams and panicked cries were softer and less frequent until none could be heard at all. With all the noise, Martina wasn't surprised that no one stopped them from slipping softly away. She doubted anyone even noticed them out in the streets.

They approached the gap between two of the mountains and pushed their way through the thick vegetation. In the dark, it was hard to see all the branches that stuck out, snagging their hair and clothes as they pushed their way through. Finally, they reached the point where the flowers and vines gave way to an open field. Before them, the orchard sprawled across the land. However, rather than the peaceful field and trees from a few days ago, they were now faced with a different scene.

Every one of the trees had wilted, and the fruits appeared deflated as they hung limply, oozing a thick honey-like liquid onto the ground below. Only a few of the trees near the front seemed to have any life left in them, but they didn't look like they would last much longer. As the three got closer, they found the nymphs whom they had seen playing only a few days ago lying on the ground as if they had stopped in the middle of what they were doing and fallen asleep.

Heath squatted down and peered into one of their pallid faces. "Guys, this doesn't look good. I hope we're not too late." He slumped to the ground beside the nymph and stared out across the destruction.

Martina and London, too, squatted by the nymph. Martina touched the nymph's hand. "It feels warm. And she still has a pulse, though it seems really slow." Looking around at the trees and the sleeping nymphs, Martina frowned.

"How could this have happened?" London asked.

"I think this is too much for us to handle alone," Martina said. "We need to tell Alfwyn."

"It's like they're sleeping, but one of them should have heard us and woken up, by now." London gently shook another nymph to try to wake him.

Wandering through the orchard, the group found that all the nymphs seemed to be sleeping.

"Ew. The ground is spongy back here, guys," London called from somewhere in the middle of the trees. She gingerly picked her way back to the front of the orchard and wiped her shoes in the grass.

"But it hasn't been raining here," Martina said. "Every day has been sunny." She thought for a moment. "Isn't there a stream in here?"

"Yeah, it's at the back," Heath said. "Remember the waterfall from the other day?"

"We better check that out," Martina said. "Maybe it rained somewhere else, and it made the stream overflow."

Walking toward the back of the orchard, Martina, Heath, and London picked through the increasingly swampy ground until the mud became so thick they could walk no more. From there, they could see that the stream had indeed overflowed, but had now receded some. The grass just a few feet from the bank was all that was still under water.

"How could it have flooded so much of the orchard, done all this damage, and then gone down in just two days?" Martina said. "This orchard is huge. That's a lot of water to drain out of here."

"At least we figured out what happened to the dreaming trees," Heath said. "Not that it's a good thing, but now we know why the Rhihalven have been having nightmares. Overwatering the plants: bad idea."

"Look at how muddy the stream is at the end far from the waterfall," Martina said. "I wonder why it's like that."

"Maybe it's because of all the dirt it brought back when it receded," Heath replied.

With no actual answers, the group began walking back to the front of the orchard. As she walked, Martina eyed the destruction. Something just wasn't right. And she didn't appreciate getting her shoes muddy, either. She knew from experience with her ballet slippers that dirt didn't come out of satin easily.

"I want to know what happened to all the nymphs. How is it that they are all still dead asleep?" London said.

"They're outside of town," Heath said. "Maybe they can't hear all the screaming. Plus they don't seem to be having nightmares like the Rhihalven are."

"That does make sense, but why won't they wake up now?" Martina asked.

"Maybe they're really tired from trying to drain the orchard?" London suggested.

"Or, maybe they are hibernating," Heath said. "We don't know that nymphs don't hibernate." Heath nodded his head. "Like bears."

"I don't think they hibernate, Heath," Martina said. "They were awake when we came, and they didn't have enough fat on them for a long, hard winter." Martina stopped walking and turned to the others. "Let's say they *were* trying to drain the garden. They could have just gone to the Rhihalven and asked for help instead of exhausting themselves, right?"

"Unless they've just been sleeping all this time," Heath said.

Martina sighed. "I don't know about that. It still sounds strange. Let's just get back to Adalborg and tell Alfwyn what we found. He might have a better idea of what's going on."

As they approached the front of the garden, a strange cracking noise could be heard. Close to the exit, the vegetation looked thicker and more flowery. As they approached, the flowering plants moved as if they had been blown by a breeze.

"It doesn't seem windy in here." Martina's hair remained oddly where she had left it, rather than flipping annoyingly into her face and catching on her lip gloss.

"Are those plants moving?" London asked.

"I saw them move too," Heath said.

"They look familiar," Martina said. "I wonder if my mom has some of these at home. They look like —"

Just then, the plants sprang to life and leapt at the children. Martina realized where she had seen the plants: on the front lawn of Adalborg. "Snapdragons," she yelled.

The trio crashed through the vegetation as fast as they could. These were wild snapdragons, which probably meant that, unlike Pyra, they had not been deflamed.

As they ran, they heard the snapdragons panting behind them, coughing puffs of fire in every direction. The smell of singed vegetation permeated the air.

Martina could see the bridge just ahead in the bobbing light of Heath's flashlight. Pounding across the bridge, the three of them turned left onto a side street to lose the wild snapdragons.

The little dragons followed them across the wooden bridge.

"Maybe the bridge will catch fire from their breath," Heath panted.

But the running plants maintained the chase through the streets of Rhihalvberg.

Upon reaching the main part of town, they continued to the Head Rhihalva's house. They zigzagged clumsily through the streets and alleys, hoping to lose the snapdragons somewhere in the tangled mass of roadways, while keeping an eye toward Adalborg rising on a hillock to the east, just visible over the other buildings.

They ran through the huge fountain in Rhihalvberg's central square, but the dragons didn't seem afraid of the water and tramped through in pursuit.

"Aaaah!" Martina cried as she felt heat behind her and heard the sizzle of singed hair. "Ok, now I'm mad." She scooped up a rock from the street and lobbed it behind her. She heard a thunk that made her think she had struck a snapdragon, but relentlessly, the little dragons maintained chase and skidded around corners in pursuit.

Finally, the big wooden doors of Adalborg appeared on the hill ahead of them.

Scrambling inside Adalborg, they slammed the door just as the closest dragon snapped its jaws on the air where they had been. It blasted an angry stream of fire at the door, which survived unscathed.

Martina, Heath, and London peered out the windows.

The snapdragons paced the porch waiting for their prey to return. Stretching their jaws and emitting little puffs of smoke and fire, the dragons looked both angry and hungry. Each time a dragon saw the group gathered at the window, the dragon would rush forward and smack right into it.

Inside, they carried on in nervous whispers about their adventure.

"I wonder why those dragons were in there," Martina said. "Didn't Chavdra say the nymphs were the only creatures who live in the garden?"

"Surely there are other animals and insects, too," London said. "Chavdra might have meant creatures who have a civilization or culture or wear clothes or whatever it is that makes them count."

"I still think that those snapdragons shouldn't have been there." Martina furrowed her eyebrows, thinking. "There's something suspicious about that flood, too."

"I agree," London said.

"Remember how we sneaked out of the house and brought back a bunch of dragons?" Heath said. "Now is the time to figure out how to get rid of them. We can reminisce later."

"Good point," London said. "Any ideas?"

"Not a one," Heath answered. "I just hope they don't tear up the porch and yard. Then we would be in real trouble."

Tear up the yard? That reminded Martina of something. She dashed to the cupboard and pulled out the bag of sawdust Parisa had used on the ants.

"Snapdragons are a bit bigger, but it might work," she said.

Martina jogged up a small spiral staircase by the door that led to the deck around the observatory.

The snapdragons sprang to life again when they saw Martina on the deck. Snarling and spewing fire, they jumped at her, but only rose a couple feet off the ground.

She sprinkled the sawdust onto the sleeping snapdragons. Nothing happened.

One of them sneezed fire, but the others continued growling angrily.

"It's not working, Martina," Heath called up to her.

"I see that." Martina was at a loss.

"I think Parisa said something when she did it," Heath said. "I don't know what it was, though."

"What is going on here?" Alfwyn asked. He had entered the room in his nightclothes, the dark circles under his eyes being pronounced after several sleepless nights. His eyes were bloodshot, and he dragged his feet as he walked. "I heard a noise outside and came downstairs to see what was happening." He crossed his arms and looked suspiciously at them.

Martina came in from the deck. "We went to see the Garden of Afalonga because we thought that something might have happened to the dreaming trees that might be causing everyone's nightmares." Quickly, she explained what they saw when they arrived and how the snapdragons had chased them back to the house.

Alfwyn peered through the window to view the group of agitated snapdragons in his front yard. "It was clever of you to use Ash of Death to be rid of them." He climbed to the balcony, took the bag from Martina, and sprinkled the ash on the snapdragons, chanting an incantation. Slowly, the snapdragons faded from sight.

Alfwyn and Martina descended the stairs to join the others.

"Usually, wild snapdragons do not come so close to town, let alone *into* town," Alfwyn said. "And the nymphs do not hibernate, sorry Heath, or sleep that soundly." He replaced the Ash of Death in the drawer.

"Are the snapdragons dead?" London asked. She was ever a champion for animal rights.

"No, they simply returned to the forest where they are supposed to be," Alfwyn said. "It doesn't hurt them. It is called 'Ash of Death' because the tree it comes from is the Melitama – the Death Tree. The Melitama does not grow leaves, so it always looks dead." Alfwyn shook his head and smiled tiredly. "Now, we need to see what's wrong with the garden." Alfwyn donned one of several plain black cloaks from the hall closet and led the group out the front door.

Upon returning to the Garden of Afalonga, they found that nothing had changed in the short time since they'd been there. The trees were still dripping with golden juices, and the nymphs were still sleeping on the ground.

Alfwyn bent to check on one of the nymphs.

"Something is definitely odd here. Look at this." He pointed at the ground where some half-eaten crackers with jelly lay crumbled and soggy. "I wonder . . ." He stood and circled a few of the other nymphs, finding more cracker crumbs on the ground and on their hands. "They fell asleep while they were eating," Alfwyn said. "I suspect these nymphs have been given a sleeping potion."

Walking over to the entrance, he dug through the vines and then pointed to a flowering plant. "The leaves of this plant, the Ahypnos Morning Glory, can be used to brew a tea that will awaken anyone. It works well for counteracting sleeping potions."

With that, Alfwyn conjured a water-filled cauldron and a fire. He brewed the tea and left it to Martina, Heath, and London to administer to all the nymphs, while he set to work on the trees. Luckily, the weather Rhihalva had painted a full moon that night, making it easy to see with magical light.

The tea took its effect slowly on the nymphs, making them sit up groggily and stare glassy-eyed for a long time, mumbling in confusion.

With each tree, Alfwyn spent only a moment repairing all the fruits. He gently cupped one, closed his eyes, and spoke under his breath. Soon all the fruits on that tree were plump and glittering in the moonlight, the dreams intact safely inside.

"His powers are amazing," Martina thought. She moved to another nymph and gently tipped the cup to his mouth. "I could solve problems so easily if I could do that."

Eventually, Alfwyn began pulling the water from the saturated ground, dragging his arms in a scooping action over and over again. He made a cloud over the garden with the extra water and gradually sent it over the mountains toward the Swamp of Sorrows.

Slowly, the garden began to look as it had several days before. The healthy fruits sparkled as the first rays of sunlight poured in through the gaps in the mountains.

Once everything seemed to be under control and the nymphs had fully awakened, Alfwyn approached a group of three who had risen and were now toweling off and chattering confusedly about why they were sleeping on the ground. "Moonbud, did you see how this happened to the garden?" he asked one of them.

In a soft feathery voice, the nymph spoke. "Sweetglow, Sugarberry, and I were just checking some of the trees to be sure they had enough water when the whole garden grew very dark. Frogspaz was serving our evening meal, so we got our food and continued with what we had been doing before." She turned to the three humans. "We do not usually sit down to eat, as you do."

Alfwyn nodded weakly with encouragement, his exhaustion starting to show again. Moonbud continued, "As we ate, we started feeling very sleepy. Soon, I was yawning and collapsed on the ground. It was so comfortable I guess I fell asleep. And now, it looks like everyone else had the same problem." She gestured around at the other nymphs standing up and stretching.

"Did you happen to see the dreaming trees rotting or the flood?" Martina asked.

"The garden was fine when I fell asleep," Moonbud said. "But when I first awoke, it was as you saw it: a mess." The nymph spread her tiny arms. "I don't know anything else."

"You undoubtedly were given a sleeping potion," Alfwyn said. "I will have to speak with Frogspaz to see what happened before he served the crackers. We need to figure out how sleeping potion ended up in your food."

Alfwyn paused and began pacing through the garden. Suddenly, he stopped in his tracks. "I wonder if someone else gave Frogspaz the sleeping potion to distribute without him knowing it. And then, they flooded the garden. Flooding the garden with that toxic water must have killed the fruits and caused the Rhihalven to dream of the sorrows of the past. But who would want to do that? How? And why?"

"Someone who would want to *remind* all the Rhihalven of their past." The voice that made this statement came from near the entrance of the garden. Pushing the vegetation aside, Alfwyn's hairy assistant Malandros stepped from behind the bushes. "I thought these young humans would be no good from the moment I laid eyes on them. They are the ones, sir, who have flooded and destroyed the dreaming trees." Malandros brushed the twigs and leaves from his dirty, grey tunic.

"You must have some reason to make a statement like that, Malandros." Alfwyn stepped forward and spread his arms in a gesture of protecting them. "These humans would not have intentionally harmed the Rhihalven."

"You and I both know that these humans *would* harm the Rhihalven, do we not, Alfwyn?" Malandros stepped forward menacingly. "Everyone in Rhihalvberg knows the dangers that humans pose. Admit it. Humans have always been a danger. Our government has been too weak to do anything about it, much less to let the rest of the Rhihalven know what has happened in the past."

"Our government has always made the right decisions about our relations with the humans," Alfwyn said. "They have not posed a threat to us for more than 40,000 years."

"However," Malandros said, "until the past few days, no one knew the truth of exactly how bad it was before. Who knows what destruction these three will wreak on our fellow Rhihalven after seeing what they have done to our dreaming trees." Malandros shook his fist. "The truth has been revealed. The peace we experienced for many thousands of years has been a dream. But we now know that the dreams of the past may well reveal to us the reality of the future." Malandros stepped forward again and held out his open palm. "Step aside, Alfwyn. Stop defending the threat that will destroy us all."

"I will never let them be harmed, Malandros," Alfwyn said. "Return to Rhihalvberg, and get some rest. It is obvious that all of us have become paranoid from the lack of good sleep. Martina, Heath, and London were the ones who told me of the destruction. As you can see, they have helped me to set it right." He motioned toward the garden which had been fully returned to its original beauty.

"You leave me no choice, then, you gullible fool." Malandros held up his hand. "If I must, I shall fight you to get to them." He began shouting spells and waving his hand in Alfwyn's direction.

"Achofore," Malandros yelled. The air sizzled with the curse as it zinged toward Alfwyn.

"Munduido," Alfwyn cried. He whooshed his arms through the air.

"Over here." A tiny hand clamped around Martina's wrist and pulled her toward the trees. "Alfwyn just said a life-protecting spell. This can't be good."

Martina dashed for the cover of the trees along with Heath, London, and any nymphs in the area.

"Askleparus," Malandros said.

"Pradima," Alfwyn responded.

Spell after spell whizzed straight towards Alfwyn, but he deflected them with spells that he wielded accurately toward Malandros. They circled each other ominously, calling out curses.

"Fir-zah." Malandros directed a ball of light directly at Alfwyn's head.

It was deflected as Alfwyn yelled "bergo," but Malandros suddenly fell to the ground as he caught the edge of the reflected curse, which singed off a gob of his unkempt hair.

Martina peered out between the branches as she waited. She wanted so badly to help Alfwyn. "Hey," she whispered to one of the nymphs, "why aren't you helping?"

"Our magic is very weak, and only gardening-related," whispered the nymph. "The best I could do is toss a branch in there. They are better off taking care of this alone."

As Malandros struggled to get back up, Alfwyn glanced back toward the trees where they were all hiding.

Martina saw Malandros pull his arm back as if he were preparing to pitch a baseball. She gasped.

Alfwyn realized too late that Malandros was recovering. Consequently, his next deflecting spell missed its mark, and the full shock of the curse that Malandros flung at him dug deep into his right calf. The flesh tore, and he collapsed onto the ground. As he fell, his outstretched palm aimed directly at the now smirking Malandros. Alfwyn uttered "Stamacia," which caused Malandros to fall into a catatonic stupor.

As Malandros froze, a figure wearing a dark cape leapt from the top of a tree that was in complete shadow. His face was hidden by a hood pulled low. Only his pale hand stood out clearly in the darkness. Reaching out, the figure uttered "waddan," and then vanished along with Malandros's body.

Running from behind the tree, the trio hurried to Alfwyn's side. Nymphs from everywhere in the garden rushed to the aid of the Head Rhihalva.

"Are you okay?" Martina asked. She eyed the blood oozing from the gash in Alfwyn's leg.

"Oh, that?" Alfwyn sat up. "I just need to get back to the house to fix it. It is nothing." Alfwyn brushed the dirt from his torn pants leg. He tried to stand up, but the pressure on his leg must have been too much.

Martina, Heath, and London tried to help Alfwyn, but he insisted the walk back would be too long. Reaching into his pocket, Alfwyn pulled out what looked like a fifty-cent piece. He pressed his thumb into the center of the silver coin until it turned a vivid green. Then, he put the coin back in his pocket. "I always keep a grígorpal on me for emergencies. It is for the Head Rhihalva's use only and has gotten me out of many jams."

As soon as the words were out of his mouth, Chavdra came rushing through the plants at the entrance of the garden. Quickly, she helped Alfwyn to a seat of the Lollie Trolley and waited for them all to sit down. In a flash, she floated the trolley to the front door of the Head Rhihalva's house.

Once they were inside, Parisa and the Rhihalva children came downstairs. "Where have you been? Oh, my goodness," Parisa exclaimed as soon as she saw Alfwyn's leg. "What happened?"

"I will be fine." Alfwyn sat down.

Parisa ran to the kitchen and returned carrying a small jar. "Not a word out of you until I fix that cut," she said. "It looks terribly deep. Hold still." Parisa opened the jar and sprinkled something powdery onto the cut on Alfwyn's leg. The gash began to close and immediately stopped bleeding. But it didn't heal completely. "This may not be good enough for something of that nature. You may have to let it completely heal naturally. Now tell me what you did to get this." Parisa sat down opposite him. With their children seated on the couch and looking more awake than they had in days, Alfwyn began recounting the adventures of the night to his family. He finished with his fight with Malandros.

As Alfwyn talked, Martina absentmindedly picked up the bottle of powder. It was marked "Elavidis." Martina marveled at its capability to heal all wounds. If only it could have healed that ancient rift between the humans and Rhihalven. Something about these prehistoric fights must have bothered Malandros enough to come after Martina, Heath, and London. Martina wondered if Malandros had been telling the truth in the garden. Did everyone really believe that they were behind the nightmares?

Chapter 8 – A Soggy Suspect

By late that afternoon, Martina, Heath, and London had caught up on some of their sleep. While Alfwyn fielded questions in his office from all the major Rhihalven newspapers about what had happened in the garden, they shut themselves in their room and discussed the strange appearance and disappearance of Malandros.

"It really bothers me that he thinks we were the ones who caused the flood," Martina said. "W*hy* he would think that?"

"I think he was just trying to blame us because *he* was the one who did it," Heath said.

Martina was aware of Heath's conspiracy theories and other crazy ideas. Although, ever since the ice cream machine had opened for them, she admitted that she needed to look at Heath's suggestions—bizarre as they may seem—a little more seriously. Still, she couldn't make the connection.

"There isn't any evidence to point to anyone, though," Martina said. "Frogspaz told Alfwyn he bought jelly from a different peddler than the usual one, but he couldn't remember what the guy looked like." Martina paused, deep in thought. "What was going on the night all the nightmares started?"

"That was the night of the awful puppet show," Heath said. "I'm surprised that sort of thing hadn't given the Rhihalven nightmares before." He poked London in the ribs with his elbow. She snickered in response.

Martina rolled her eyes. "That *was* the night of the puppet show, and practically everyone in town was there. That would give someone the perfect opportunity to go to the garden and do some damage." She stopped suddenly.

"Everyone was there, *except* Malandros," London said.

"That's what I was just thinking," Martina said. "He got up in the middle of the first act and didn't come back until intermission."

"He doesn't have an alibi," Heath practically sang. "I knew he was the one who did it. We have to tell Alfwyn." He jumped up and headed for the door as he spoke.

"We don't have any real proof, though," Martina said. "The nymphs didn't see him there. And other Rhihalven might not have been at the puppet show either, so that doesn't mean that he did it." Again, she was silent as she thought about how they could solve the problem. She wanted so badly to believe that Malandros *was* the one who had done the damage, so they could clear their names.

"What about motive?" London began. "Why would he have caused a flood? All it did was keep the Rhihalven from sleeping well. It would have affected Malandros that way, too."

"I wouldn't put it past him to use magic to cause the flood," Heath said. "Then he blames us because we are outsiders. No one here can say we wouldn't do something like that because they don't know us that well."

"On the same note, Heath," Martina said, "we don't know Malandros well enough to say that he is definitely the one who did it. Maybe we just got a bad impression of him the night he brought us to our room. Maybe he coincidentally wasn't there the night the nightmares started," she reminded him.

"But he didn't bother to see what we were like before he blamed us for the flooding," Heath said. "So why should we get to know him first? If he's going to jump to conclusions just because we are humans, then why shouldn't we blame him because he comes across as evil?"

"Heath, calm down," London said. "We'll figure it out, okay."

"But he doesn't come across as *evil*," Martina said. "Try to see it from his point of view. He's concerned about someone hurting—"

Someone knocked on the door, cutting her off. Siofra entered the room followed by another Alvar member.

Martina smiled at them, but they were not smiling.

"We need to speak to you all downstairs," Siofra stated. "I am afraid we have a lot of things to clear up. Follow me please."

Worried, Martina, Heath, and London followed Siofra to the Head Rhihalva's office. When they arrived, they found several reporters there, along with Alfwyn, Parisa, and their children.

Bits of a conversation about a break in at the chemist's shop drifted toward the trio as they entered. Martina feared they were about to be blamed for it, too.

Parisa rushed over to them and hugged them close. She whispered, "Do not worry. We will find a way out of this mess."

Puzzled, they nodded and turned toward Alfwyn who was waiting for them at his desk.

"A fear has been circulating through Rhihalvberg over the past few days that I was not aware of until today," Alfwyn said. "As you all know, I was first introduced to this fear early this morning when Malandros confronted me about it." Alfwyn stopped and looked hard at them. "I have been apprehensive about telling you this. I must tell you now so you will fully understand what is happening."

Alfwyn cleared his throat. "The Rhihalven know very little about life before Sheardland. We have worked hard to suppress that past because it was so terrifying. That means they know very little about humans." Alfwyn leaned back against his desk, taking the weight off his injured leg. "The only contact they have had in a very long time has been with Artemidoros Willoughby over the past fifty years. The dreams that all the Rhihalven have been having over the past few nights, which you called 'nightmares,' were about how the humans had fought with and tortured the early Rhihalven before we came to Sheardland."

London gasped.

Shifting, Alfwyn continued. "I was hesitant to tell you because I did not want you to think *I* thought humans would still attack Rhihalven. I do not know how everyone came to have the same horrible nightmares all at once. Some in Rhihalvberg believe these nightmares are not only revealing the past to them but also the future." Alfwyn nodded slowly. "They believe their fate has come full circle and that, ultimately, we have failed to outrun destruction by the humans."

"Oh no," Martina whispered.

"Consequently," Alfwyn explained, "I have consulted the Rhihalva Council as to the situation. You see, Malandros and many, many other Rhihalven believe you caused the destruction in the Garden of Afalonga, probably because of those dreams. I would like to give you the chance to speak to the Rhihalven and the other magical races of Sheardland through our newspapers, so they will understand your true role in this situation." Alfwyn extended his arm toward the back of the room. "That is why the reporters are here—to hear your side of the story." He smiled.

Martina thought Heath still looked agitated from their discussion earlier, so she didn't want to give him the opportunity to tell the Rhihalven just how crazy he thought Malandros was. She spoke first.

"We didn't mean any harm by visiting here," Martina said. "We actually ended up here by accident." Martina continued to babble nervously to the reporters about how they had come across the entrance to Sheardland. Rushing on through their story, Martina talked about the night of the puppet show and how they had been there the whole time.

Alfwyn smiled and nodded, confirming the story.

The reporters scribbled furiously as Martina spoke, jotting notes with their quills as Martina came to the end of what had happened in the garden.

Finally, one of the reporters asked Alfwyn, "What do you think of the matter?"

"As you can see," he replied, "they have an alibi for where they were the night that the nightmares began." He waited as the reporter made notes on his pad. "The only unresolved problem now is that Malandros has completely disappeared. Siofra has the Alvar searching every last corner of Sheardland, but they have come up with nothing. And no one knows who the mysterious Rhihalva was in the garden."

"Once he is found," Siofra said, "Malandros will pay the ultimate penalty for the worst crime one could possibly commit. An attempt to injure the Head Rhihalva is one of the most unforgivable things a Rhihalva can do." She bowed in Alfwyn's direction. "The same follows for every culture here. We respect our leaders."

"If you don't mind my asking, Sir," Martina said to Alfwyn, "what is the punishment for such a crime?"

"Crimes here are so rare," Alfwyn began. "However, the Rhihalva responsible for such mischief is always banished."

"Where do you banish them?" London asked. She looked relieved that they had been cleared.

"To the surface," Alfwyn answered.

As Martina looked at her friends' faces, she could tell they were just as shocked as she was. It made her wonder how many Rhihalven were walking among the humans. Had some of the world's greatest crimes been committed by magic?

"The fear of the unknown human world is usually enough of a threat to deter crime," Alfwyn continued. "I guess Malandros's fear of the humans being here and destroying us was greater than his fear of being sent to the surface."

"He *actually* thought that the three of us were going to destroy the Rhihalven? Us?" Heath ranted. "Does he even know anything about humans? We don't have magic powers. Rhihalven could kick our butts in, like, a millisecond. How stupid."

Alfwyn attempted to calm him by saying, "Those who have gotten to know you understand that this is not plausible. When Malandros saw you three in the garden, he must have assumed that your being there implicated you."

Finally, one of the reporters spoke up. "Do you think that the damage to the dreaming trees is related to the recent break-ins at the chemist's shop?"

"I am suspicious of the large amounts of sleeping draughts missing," Alfwyn answered, "but it bears further investigation. There may be a connection between the jelly that was used to put the nymphs in the garden to sleep and the robbery." Leaning heavily on his desk, Alfwyn stood up. "Thank you. That will be all for the time being. I would greatly appreciate it if a full account could go into each of the papers. It is very important that there is no misunderstanding about the humans. Who knows what sort of chaos would erupt if the inhabitants of Sheardland thought we were truly in danger?"

The reporters filed out of the office and climbed aboard the Lollie Trolley, which was waiting just outside Adalborg. Breathing a sigh of relief, the Branimirs and Martina, Heath, and London all stared blankly at each other.

Martina was sure everyone was suffering from sheer mental exhaustion.

"I know this looks like it has all been resolved," Alfwyn said, "but I would like for you all to remain inside for the time being. I would not want someone who has not read the paper to panic and try to senselessly defend themselves against you when you are not going to cause them harm." He laughed. "Why not go upstairs with the boys and play a game for awhile? I need to handle the situation at the chemist's."

"I will be in my studio if anyone needs me," Parisa said. She hugged them again. Then, scooping up Ilona, she left the office.

Following the triplets up the stairs to their bedroom, Martina tried to catch London's eye. When London finally looked her way, Martina mouthed the words, "We have to find out who stole that sleeping draught."

"How can we lose the boys?" London mouthed back.

"Wait until we start playing the game," Martina whispered. "I have an idea."

When they arrived at the triplets' room, the boys got out the supplies they needed to play the game. Haldor set a two-foot-high cone in the center of the room and explained how to play.

"It might be difficult for you because you cannot do magic, but we will help you," he said excitedly. "This game is called 'Zenith.' When it is your turn, you draw a card, and it tells you how far up the mountain you can go."

"And then, if you get pushed back," Torvald added, "someone else has to think of a way to save you."

"So, how do you win?" Heath asked.

"That is the best part," Brantrod said. "The game is over when we all reach the top at the same time. So we all get to win *together*. No one loses."

"Oh, that sounds like fun," London said skeptically.

"You know, I'm still tired." Martina nodded her head slowly while she attempted telepathy with London. "I'm going to take a nap until dinner. How about you guys?"

"Yeah," London replied, faking a yawn. "I don't know how much longer I can keep my eyes open."

"Well, I'm good," Heath said. London and Martina shot him looks that made him aware of his ignorance. "I mean, gosh, I'm tired. I could use some extra sleep."

"Aw, that is too bad," Torvald said. "This is one of the best games ever."

The other two nodded.

"Maybe we can play later," Haldor said.

"Uh, yeah, later is good," Martina called behind her as she left the room followed by London and Heath. Once they reached their bedroom, she hurriedly shut the door. "How can we get out of here without being seen?"

"More importantly, what are we doing?" Heath demanded. "Why do we need to avoid being seen? Ooh! Are we going to track down Malandros?"

"Not yet," Martina said. "We have to find out who stole that sleeping draught."

"Why does that matter?" Heath said. "We've already been cleared of all the stuff that happened in the garden, so it's not our problem." He crossed over to his bed and sat down.

"Actually, I think it might still be our problem," Martina said. "And even if it wasn't, shouldn't we try to help? This might be related to whatever Mr. Willoughby discovered down here. Maybe that's the real reason Malandros accused us of causing the nightmares and the destruction. Maybe he doesn't want us around to find out the same thing Mr. Willoughby did."

"If everyone believes that we did it," London said, "then Malandros can get away with everything he's done, even if it has nothing to do with whatever it is Mr. Willoughby discovered."

"We need to find out what that is," Heath said. "I'm getting tired of not knowing."

"Ha! I agree," Martina said. "So what would happen to us if everyone believed that we caused the problems?" she prodded.

"Everyone would probably hate us," Heath said, "and we would get kicked out of Sheardland because they would think we were going to attack them." He crossed his arms.

"Exactly," Martina said. "So if we want to be allowed to stay here, we had better start looking for evidence that proves our innocence. And that means starting with who stole the sleeping draughts."

"The boys would be powerful allies in this, Martina," Heath interjected. "They can do magic, and they know where everything is."

"I don't know," London interrupted. "I think we should leave them out of it. They don't exactly seem adventurous."

"That's true," Martina said. "And we would have to catch them up on everything, which would take forever. So—"

"So what are we doing hanging out here?" Heath stalked toward the door. "Let's get moving."

"We have to figure out—" Martina started to say.

"Ah, too slow, Watson," Heath said. "We're moving out." He opened the door and jogged down the stairs to the balcony above the foyer. Martina and London looked at each other worriedly and ran after him.

Arriving at the landing, they were surprised to see that Siofra and several members of the Alvar had already returned from their investigation. Quickly,

Martina and London joined Heath and ducked behind some potted plants that were perched near the railing.

" . . . but she said that by the time she returned from the puppet show," Siofra reported, "there was so much water in the basement that she made everything float in mid-air to keep it from being ruined. Then she returned to the shop on the main floor. There, she noticed that every ounce of sleeping draught was gone. The only evidence we found were some stains from recent water damage to the floor, plus the blodwen honey candy and sleeping draughts that were missing." Siofra had apparently finished her report.

"No footprints, no fingerprints, no hairs? Nothing else?" Alfwyn queried.

"Nothing whatsoever," Siofra replied.

"Candy and water damage, huh? That is very strange." Alfwyn seemed to ponder the predicament. Finally, he said, "I will be in my office. Please check with neighbors to see if anyone saw someone leaving the shop that day after it was closed."

As Alfwyn went to his office, the Alvar left.

Martina's eyes grew wide as she put the pieces together. "It really seems like Malandros is behind all of this," she said. "After he left the puppet show, he flooded the chemist's shop to get the sleeping draught, and then he flooded the garden after he used the draught on the nymphs."

"I don't understand why Malandros hates us so much," Heath said, "but the rest of it makes perfect sense. And I'm glad you're starting to agree with me. My crazy ideas aren't so crazy, eh? What's the plan now?"

Martina smiled. "The Alvar investigated the scene of the crime, and it's in our best interest to find out what they discovered. Let's ask Alfwyn what else Siofra told him." She stood and headed for Alfwyn's office.

Heath and London followed her.

Once inside the office, the three lost no time in recounting everything they had been thinking about the robbery and the disaster in the garden.

Alfwyn nodded and stroked his beard thoughtfully. "I am certainly glad you did not try to follow the Alvar to the chemist's shop. The newspapers are not out yet, and you might not have been met with much benevolence in the street." He leaned back in his chair. "I understand why you would think that Malandros is responsible for all of this. However, I cannot be certain, myself, that he is. His guilt is not completely evident from what we have found."

"What do you mean?" Heath said. "Isn't it obvious he's the one who flooded the chemist's shop and the Garden? And he stole the sleeping draughts to drug the nymphs?"

"Not necessarily," Alfwyn began. "Puddles of water were on the floor, and Rhihalven cannot control water with their magic. Also, blodwen honey candy was missing along with the sleeping draughts. Why would Malandros have stolen the candy? He has a job and could have easily bought it."

"Then why would he steal the sleeping draft?" Heath asked. "Couldn't he buy it, too?"

"People steal stuff all the time," London said.

"People do, but Rhihalven do not," Alfwyn said. "You have to have a prescription for the sleeping draught, so it is harder to come by."

"OK, that makes sense," Martina said.

"But there is no logical reason for him to take that candy," Alfwyn continued. "What confuses me is that there is a creature known to be unable to resist ... no, never mind. That is totally impossible. He would not have stolen the candy." Alfwyn shook his head. "The important thing is that Rhihalven and other inhabitants of Sheardland cannot control water like that. So Malandros could not have used *magic* to cause the flooding."

"So who did it?" Martina asked. "Who can control water with their magic?"

"It is not a question of 'who' but of 'what.'" Alfwyn leaned forward. "There is a legend about something called the Diana's Eye which can control water. Whoever has been responsible for the floods may have run across this stone somehow and used it. But I am not certain that the answer is so easy."

"Why do you think that?" Martina asked.

"It was Malandros," Heath said, "and he did it to make everyone hate us, so we would be banished." He sported a smug smile.

"That sounds like it would make sense, but Malandros could not have been the one to steal the sleeping draughts," Alfwyn said. "He would not have left water on the floor because it wasn't raining and nothing was spilled or leaking—unless of course, he somehow had the Diana's Eye, which I think is unlikely. And as I have said, he would not have stolen the candy. If he intended to steal the sleeping draught, he would have stolen it and left without bothering with the candy. Rhihalven, by nature, are not easily distracted from a task at hand." Alfwyn looked pensive.

They leaned closer to the desk and waited for him to conclude.

"The only explanation—and I admit it is a strange one—is that the Sychateros stole it," Alfwyn said. "They are partially-amphibious—which would explain the water—and they have a high-sugar diet, which helps them stay warm in the water. They may have stolen the candy to maintain their diet." Alfwyn scratched his head. "It does not fit in with everything else that has happened, though. They would still need the Diana's Eye to flood the Garden, but what would they gain by it? And, there is the problem of their existence." Alfwyn glanced across the room at his bookshelves. "Let me check on something."

Martina, Heath, and London waited. Martina wondered what strange secrets were about to be revealed to them.

Chapter 9 - The Storage Room for Unknown Secrets

Alfwyn pushed himself out of the chair very carefully, likely protecting his injured leg. He didn't even wince, but Martina did. Limping slightly, he made his way across the chamber to a set of bookshelves built into the wall. Not one of the books could have been printed within the last hundred years or could have weighed less than twenty pounds. And every one of them was peeling and gave off a distinct smell of mold.

Alfwyn selected a particularly crusty volume and proceeded to the table nearby. The gold lettering on the spine still shone faintly with the title of the book: "Legends and Myths of Sheardland." He placed it on the book holder and gently turned the yellowed pages with gloved hands.

Martina, Heath, and London gathered around the book holder and squeezed in close to the book.

"Here it is," Alfwyn said. "This is what the Diana's Eye is supposed to look like." He read the caption below the drawing. "'Diana's Eye (see figure one), one of eight such stones, is located at equidistant points on the Earth. The location of each of these stones is known by no one but is kept locked in the Rhihalva Hall of Knowledge. If any of the stones is moved from its position, the moon will sway in its orbit, causing a change in the tides. An Eye will pull on any water in its vicinity. If the shift in the stone's position is significant enough or if more than one stone is moved, the effect could be catastrophic.'"

The picture above the caption looked like a large cat's eye marble, about the size of a baseball, with a deep purple streak through the middle of its translucent, silvery glass orb. Strangely, though, it almost looked alive. Martina knew if she closed her eyes, she could imagine it blinking. She glanced away at the thought.

"It sounds like if the tides are off balance, it might cause flooding," London deduced.

"That must be why there has been so much flooding in southern Asia," Martina said. She finally put together the reason behind the huge waves and massive damage. Her family had heard so much about it on the news.

"I was not aware of that, but, yes, that could be caused by the stone being moved," Alfwyn turned a page in the book and began perusing the ancient text.

"Maybe the Sychateros wanted to flood Asia," London said. She tried to read over Alfwyn's shoulder.

Alfwyn turned to face them. "Perhaps they wanted to create a place to live outside of Sheardland."

"But why would anyone want to leave Sheardland?" Heath asked. "You don't have to deal with bad weather or natural disasters, and most of the

Rhihalven we've met have been so nice." Heath paused. "Except Malandros, of course."

"Well, it was not the Sychateros' idea to come here in the first place," Alfwyn answered. "The Rhihalven convinced them to do so. Sychateros are a very weak species. Everything they ever accomplished they were convinced to do by other, stronger creatures." Alfwyn closed the book and replaced it on the shelf. He paced the length of the room slowly, stroking his beard and twisting the strands around his hand.

"What are the Sychateros like?" asked London.

Continuing to pace, Alfwyn answered her. "They are husky, humanoid, semi-aquatic creatures with both gills and lungs. In fact, their name means 'twice-breathing.' When they are in the water, their lungs act as an air bladder, and when they are in the open air, the gills close to allow the lungs to get oxygen. When the Rhihalven first came here, we tried to convince all the other magical beings that they should come with us. With the rise of the humans, we felt that we had no choice. Humans would never understand that our magic would not be used to overpower them."

"Humans never trust magic," London added. "That's why the Salem Witch Trials happened."

"Right, and that is just one example of what we knew would happen if we stayed," Alfwyn said. "That was why we created this place. It was a safe way to be near the humans to make sure they would not unknowingly destroy the Earth and to make sure we could still have the lifestyle we were accustomed to." Alfwyn stopped and gazed out the window. "We convinced the other creatures to come for the same reasons. The Sychateros were some of the first to agree with us that the move needed to take place. Once we were ready, we moved everyone to Sheardland. We had separate areas for each species according to their needs."

"How did you do that?" Heath asked.

"Our powerful cartographer drew the regions on her map, and they were created." Alfwyn stopped pacing and returned to the bookshelves. He pulled an especially lengthy volume marked "History of the Beings of Sheardland, Volume 3, R–Z" from one of the lower shelves and carried the burgundy book to another book holder.

Once again, Martina, Heath, and London gathered around.

Alfwyn flipped to a page titled "History of the Sychateros Species."

A knock sounded at the door. "Excuse me, Lord Branimir," said the Alvar warrior who poked his head in, "some reporters from Trevtisis and Aoibrún would like a word with you and a quote about the ordeal in the Garden."

"Please pardon me a moment," Alfwyn said to the trio. "The Fairies and Trolls must be interested in our latest news."

As soon as Alfwyn was gone, Martina turned to the others. "Clearly, the word has gotten out. Let's find out what we can while we wait." She stared at the drawings of Sychateros and their habitat on the first pages of the section. A shudder crept through her. They certainly were creepy. Martina flipped the page to keep from looking at them.

"What's this?" Martina picked up several leaves of paper folded together between the pages of the book. At the top of the first was the title, 'Investigation into Missing Species: Sychateros.'

"I wonder what happened," London said.

"The Sychateros region," Martina read, "was of a sufficient size and had plenty of water to provide for their needs. The one thing we did not foresee was their jealousy of each other."

"I bet they were jealous of the ugliest Sychateros," Heath said. "The guy in the book looked proud of his lumpy head and saggy chins."

The girls laughed.

"Sychateros always need to argue with someone," Martina continued to read. "Once we provided them with their part of the world, they no longer needed to fight with other species for land and food."

"So, they began fighting among themselves?" London asked.

"One after another," Martina read, "the Sychateros killed each other in an attempt to own all the land that had been provided for them. Twice, we sent negotiators to convince the Sychateros to end their warlike ways and to let them know that if they needed more land, our cartographer would draw more for them. But they stubbornly refused and even became angry with the Rhihalva government for interfering." She paused.

"Why would they refuse more land if that was what they wanted to begin with?" Heath said.

"That doesn't make sense to me either," Martina said. She continued reading the report. "We soon discovered that the Sychateros did not want or need more land for their species. They just did not want one Sychatero to have more land than another."

"This sounds like a soap opera." London giggled.

"Or the snobby kids at school," Heath said. "My locker is bigger, *and* I don't have to share it," he squeaked in falsetto, with his hands planted on his hips.

This brought more giggling from the girls.

"Listen to this," Martina said. "If one had more land, then the others would try to take it from him, which usually ended in the death of one or more Sychateros. Then, those who survived took his land, and the process started over. Their numbers soon dwindled from these slaughters." Martina laid down the report and leaned against a table, reflecting on what she just read. The group remained silent for a couple minutes.

"But couldn't they see that they were going to kill everyone eventually?" Heath asked. He sat down at a chair beside the table.

"That was the whole report. I don't know," Martina answered.

"According to this book," London said, "Sychateros are not very smart creatures." She dragged her hand down the page as she read. "It says 'they only know what they can quickly see. They are creatures of action, not thought.'"

"So they wouldn't have realized they could end their own species," Martina said. "Even after they were told so. Brilliant."

"The Sychateros are driven by material desire, not love for each other," London read.

"So the evidence made the Rhihalven think that the Sychateros completely wiped themselves out," Heath said. "But now the robbery in the chemist's shop and the destruction of the dreaming trees made Alfwyn think that they are still around." He interlocked his fingers and leaned back in the chair.

Alfwyn re-entered the room, his tunic fluttering as he walked. "My apologies. Now, where were we?"

"Where did the Sychateros used to live?" Martina asked. "Can you just check to see if any of them are still living there, and then question them?"

"That would be a good idea, except we do not know where they used to live." Alfwyn hobbled over to a huge map hanging on the wall.

It spanned the length of the room, from floor to ceiling. Most of the map was criss-crossed by streets, with a fair amount of forests, rivers, and mountains. The thick paper was a light cream color, crumbling slightly at the edges.

"The Elves live up here, the Rhihalven live here, the Ogres live here, and so on." As Alfwyn spoke, he gestured to the different regions of the map. "These regions are marked because Elves and Rhihalven and Ogres still exist."

"I don't get it," Heath said.

"It means that if the Sychateros were still living where they were given a place to live," Alfwyn began, "then they would show up on the map. No Sychateros live in the Sychatero area anymore, so it does not exist. And when we knew they were extinct, we removed them from the internal magic of the map. They will never show up here again." Alfwyn stepped back from the map to get a better look at it.

"Why don't we look at some older maps to see where they used to live?" Martina hoped Alfwyn would unroll some more huge maps so they could see how much Sheardland had changed over the years.

"That would be a good idea," Alfwyn began, "if there actually were old maps."

"Do you guys throw them away?" Heath asked. "Don't you have to keep a record of where stuff was?"

Alfwyn smiled for the first time since they had started talking about the Sychateros. "We have always used this one map since the beginning of this civilization. When our cartographer draws a street on her map, the street becomes real. When she marks off a region for a new group or adds a lot for a new family, it appears on the street where it has been drawn. Similarly, once a house is emptied of its inhabitants or a species dies off, the place where it once was disappears from our map."

"Wow, that's amazing," Martina said. "Can we watch her draw on the map next time she comes here?"

"She doesn't draw on this map," Alfwyn said. "She has a smaller map magically connected to this one, and the adjustments are made at the same time.

But since she does not remove areas herself, we do not know where the Sycateros used to live. And no one remembers. Everyone who lives in Sheardland has a vague connection to the Forian Tree, which has a connection to this map. The Forian Tree is the support, the earth and sky for Sheardland."

"So if the Forian Tree finds out that a creature doesn't exist because they aren't on the map, no one remembers the creatures?" Martina asked.

"Yes," Alfwyn answered. "Therefore, the place simply does not exist anymore. In fact, that is why we thought that they had killed themselves off, because the area they lived in disappeared from the map." He pointed. "You see here. There is nothing beyond what we have drawn here on the map. Once you walk to the edge of this cliff," he indicated a line at the bottom of the map, "there is nothing else. If the Sychateros have moved, we will never know because they did not request land to be added."

"Then how will we ever know if the Sychateros were the ones who took the Diana's Eye?" London finally asked, obviously bewildered.

"You must search the place where the Diana's Eye was hidden to find signs of who stole it," Alfwyn said matter-of-factly.

Martina, Heath, and London stared at each other. Finally, Heath spoke up again. "If you have never seen the stone, and no one knows where it is supposed to be, then where do we look for it?"

Alfwyn stood again. "I will take you to the Rhihalva Hall of Knowledge to retrieve the information. This is what confuses me most. The only place where the record is kept is in the Hall of Knowledge, but someone was able to find out where the Diana's Eye was hidden. All of our greatest secrets have always been kept at the Hall. We found that a secret is best kept when no one knows it, you see. Yet, nothing has been noted as missing from the Hall, and no break-ins have been reported."

"Maybe it was an inside job," Heath suggested excitedly.

"Unlikely, but possible," Alfwyn said. "The Storage Room for Unknown Secrets is charmed so no one can enter without permission. When someone gets permission to enter the room, a record is kept with the names and times of all who enter. With all the guards and spells around that room, it is impossible for anyone other than Hall workers to gain access without the Rhihalven Council knowing. They have all the records."

"The Storage Room for Unknown Secrets might not have been broken into, though," Martina said. "Maybe someone found the Diana's Eye accidentally."

"Whoever found it had to know what it was, though," Alfwyn said. "It would not be somewhere that someone could just stumble upon it. All eight eyes must be on the Earth's crust, not below it. Because of this, I am certain that someone had to be looking for it." Alfwyn paused and stroked his beard again. "The Rhihalva Hall of Knowledge will be closing soon, so we must hurry."

The trio followed Alfwyn into a small room just off the main chamber. It was lit entirely by tiny points of light glowing in the rock walls. In the middle of the room was a small pond, and a beautifully carved wooden sideboard sat against the far wall under a picture labeled "Salornma the Great, Head Rhihalva." On the table, Martina saw a jar of "Glaisliór Ink" and some quills. The opposite wall, above the pond, bore only a small map of Sheardland.

Alfwyn picked up a quill, dipped it in the ink, and bent down. He wrote "Rhihalva Hall of Knowledge" on the surface of the pond. The brown ink seared through the water, making a sizzling sound, as if the words burned completely through it. The water, which was a thick, iridescent greenish-blue, gradually pulled the splotches of ink down like flecks of dirt to settle on the bottom.

As Martina peered into the water, she could barely make out the words written in Alfwyn's large, looping letters on the bottom of the pond.

Heath, London, and Martina looked at each other. Martina's imagination whizzed as she tried to think of how writing on the water was going to get them anywhere.

"Are we going swimming?" Heath asked.

"There is no time for that," Alfwyn said. He turned around and gently stepped into the murky water without taking off his shoes or rolling up his pant legs. "Follow me."

"So we just *go*?" London raised her eyebrows.

Martina knew it would take some convincing for London to get in the questionable water.

"You will not get wet, London," Alfwyn said. "Just wade in. Please hurry. We only have so long before the charm takes effect." He paused as the trio walked down into the pond. "This is called a glaisliór. It works like osmosis. Glaisliing is the fastest way to travel around Sheardland. Normally, we would take damurses —" Alfwyn's words were cut off suddenly.

Martina felt disoriented and heard a loud buzz like television snow. The next instant, they were all standing in a massive hall with a pool of colors swimming around them. In another second, there was a loud popping noise as the glaisliór and room came into focus.

"We check in over there." Alfwyn pointed to a desk near the glaisliór.

Glaisliórs nearby were zapping Rhihalven and other creatures to and from their destinations. Another Rhihalva was waiting in line for theirs and stared impatiently at the humans as they climbed out of the murky water.

Martina felt her clothes in disbelief. She really was dry.

"Not a word until we are safely out of the main room. I will do any explaining needed," Alfwyn said. He walked up to the check-in desk. They waited in line behind a pair of portly lady Fairies who were arguing with the clerk about looking up remedy spells for obesity. When the women were finally satisfied with their answer, they waddled down a corridor to the right of the desk. Alfwyn stepped up and explained to the clerk why they were there.

The woman glanced skeptically at the trio and then wrote with her quill on some parchment. She gestured vaguely toward the area behind them. "Take these passes. They will get you where you need to go."

Alfwyn directed them to a corridor opposite the desk, which was guarded by a fierce elf carrying a dagger.

The elf inspected their passes and waved them down the long winding hallway behind him.

"This leads to a labyrinth of rooms. It helps discourage intruders," Alfwyn said. He paused at the beginning of the hallway and uttered "Dirigere." Instantly, a map of the labyrinth appeared in his hands.

The group set off down the first hallway. On both sides of them, they passed many doors. Screaming and strange noises emanated from behind the door marked "Unwanted Experiments Storage Room." Rustling papers could be heard from a door further down the hall marked "Records of Sheardland's Historical Events." Ten minutes later and after many twists and turns, the group found themselves standing outside a door painted a brilliant orange that led to the Storage Room for Unknown Secrets.

Alfwyn slipped their passes into the slot in the door.

Seconds later, the door swung open, allowing the group to enter and then slammed shut immediately after they were inside. The entire room, which extended farther than they could see in every direction, contained thousands of filing cabinets in rows. The stone floor and high ceiling echoed their steps as they approached the first row.

"We are going to be here all night," Heath complained. "Please tell me you guys have the Dewey Decimal System or something."

"It is simple, Heath," Alfwyn said. "The map shows that recorded secrets involving the natural world, or the Earth's surface, lie in the fourth quadrant. All secrets involving water lie in the third row of that quadrant. And all secrets involving location are in the last three sets of cabinets of that row. They are labeled according to topic in alphabetical order." With each new set of instructions, the map adjusted to a closer view of the cabinets and, eventually, to the exact location of the secret.

"I thought that was a map of the storage room hallway." London moved closer to the map to see.

"Our cartographer charmed the map for the use of the Head Rhihalva only," Alfwyn said, "so he or she could easily enter any building anywhere and not be lost. I have found it to be quite useful over the past few years. I never can remember my way around." Alfwyn smiled and led them toward the fourth quadrant.

As they approached the fourth quadrant, the map changed to show the location of the third row. Eventually, they approached the third row and found the filing cabinets at the end.

Locating the cabinet that Diana's Eye would fall under, Alfwyn pulled the correct drawer open. He waved his hand over the folders and said "Sortos," causing them to flip quickly until the file marked "Diana's Eye" appeared. Alfwyn removed the folder and held it out for the others to see. Inside, eight different folders were marked according to the region of the world that each Eye could be found in.

"This would be much simpler electronically," Heath muttered.

"Which one do we need?" Martina asked.

"Each stone affects the opposite side of the world," Alfwyn said. "The flooding is happening in Asia, and halfway around the world is the northeastern United States."

He removed that file and handed the rest of them to Heath, who was standing against his elbow. Alfwyn opened the file, conjured a table for the folders, and perused the papers to find the secret they needed to know.

The trio gathered around him and waited patiently.

"I guess this is it," Alfwyn gestured toward a poem. "Rather than coordinates for latitude and longitude, we have been given rhymed verse.

London read the poem aloud.

"In a stream that leads to the milky sea
There lives a poor Pisces that cannot see
She will not eat or sleep a wink
Swimming always, does not blink
Keeping vigil over Earthly tides
Day or night, on she rides
One of eight combined will try
To balance the waters through her eye."

"What is that supposed to mean?" Heath said. "Can't they give directions?" He let his shoulders drop in despair.

"We do not have time to figure it out in here," Alfwyn said. "They close in fifteen minutes."

"Let's make a copy, so we can think about it," London suggested.

Alfwyn chuckled. "I am not supposed to do this, but I think this is important enough to break the rules, especially if the Diana's Eye is missing. I must take care, however, as there is a risk of this falling into the wrong hands." He gestured with his palm toward the paper and uttered "Copius." Instantly, he was holding two copies of the document.

"We better leave," Alfwyn said. "I do not think any of us want to be locked in here overnight." Alfwyn replaced the folders and lead the way to the door. The group retraced their steps and returned to the glaisliórs.

*   *   *   *   *   *

After they returned to the guest room at Adalborg, Martina, Heath, and London got ready for bed. But they didn't go to sleep right away. For a long time, they were stretched out in the middle of the floor reading the poem over and over, trying to make some sense of it.

"Is there a lake back home that might be milky?" London asked finally.

"There's one a few minutes outside of town – Scrumston Lake," Heath said. "I guess that's more *murky* than *milky* from the acid mine drainage."

"Yeah, it's also orange," Martina said. "I don't think that would be considered milky." She frowned. "Also, this poem is ancient. That stream hasn't had acid mine drainage in it until recently. Whatever it is, it would have to be something that was around when the Rhihalven first began guarding the stones."

"But the only things that would be that old are the hills and streams." London was starting to look tired. She leaned against the pile of pillows stacked by the side of the bed.

"Or the sky!" Heath suddenly sat up and grabbed the paper from the floor.

"I knew Mr. Willoughby was right," Martina said. "We did learn stuff from him that would be useful. That's the only way to explain it." She leaned over to see the paper now in front of Heath.

"Yes, Pisces is a constellation," London said. "And the milky sea, that has to be the Milky Way Galaxy." She suddenly looked more awake.

"Maybe it means in Starry Fields?" Heath added. "That's convenient if it's somewhere in the town we live in.

"Now we just have to figure out the exact spot this is directing us to." Martina looked at the other two and waited for some recognition to appear on their now blank faces. "All this tells us is that the Pisces constellation is in the Milky Way Galaxy. It doesn't tell us where the stone actually is. Maybe there is a land formation that looks like two fish tied together by their tails, just like the symbol for Pisces?"

"I guess that's possible," Heath said. "I've never seen one though. Can we go back and take a look tomorrow?"

"That's a good idea," London said. "We've been down here for several days now. In the morning, we can ask Alfwyn to have them prepare the Dechronstructive Potion. Then we can get back all these days we've lost down here, and our parents won't suspect a thing."

"Yeah, I say we go to bed," Heath said. "I'm exhausted." He collapsed onto his own bed and put the pillow over his head. Within a few minutes, he was snoring loudly into his pillow.

Soon, Martina and London, too, drifted off to sleep.

Martina's dreamed of trying to find the Diana's Eye. Every time she got close to finding the right land form or a bend in the stream or some rocks that looked just right, Heath's snoring would grow particularly loud. Then, she would wake up just enough that she had to start over. Very close to morning, the dream changed, and she was in her own backyard. She walked toward the lake on the edge of town carrying fish food. The lake looked whitish with the billowing clouds reflected in it. Maybe that was the "milky sea." Suddenly, she awoke with a start. She knew now that they had been wrong about Pisces. The Pisces they were looking for was not a constellation, but an actual fish.

Chapter 10 - Return to the Surface

Early the next morning, Martina awoke tired but ready for the journey back home to search for the place Diana's Eye had been.

"Should we take all our stuff with us?" London asked. "We'll probably come back tonight, right?"

"I guess we should take everything," Martina said. "We probably won't need the snacks and flashlights on the return trip." She searched for the clothes she had started the journey in. "I think we should bring clean outfits with us to put on when we come back through Rhihalva Travel to Sheardland."

"Yeah, we might need to disguise ourselves as Rhihalven to trick anyone who might still be mad at us." Heath crammed several water bottles into the backpack. "Or we could bring pirate costumes back with us. It's just a thought."

"Last night, I was thinking about where the Diana's Eye might be," Martina said. "I kept dreaming about where we might find it."

"Me too," Heath said. "I dreamed that it was in the mattress here, and I tried to roll over and find it, but it kept slipping away to some other part of the mattress." He walked back over to his bed. Digging in the covers, he found what he was looking for. "I guess my socks must have come off during the night." He laughed.

"You are an unlikely princess, and that is an unlikely pea." Parisa leaned in the open doorway, smiling widely. "Are you going somewhere?"

"We have some ideas about where the Diana's Eye might be," Martina said. "Is it okay if we return to the surface today and search for it?"

"You three may come and go as you please," Parisa said. "You do not need to ask our permission." She glided into the room and placed a stack of clean clothes on the dresser for them. "I will notify the chemist to prepare Dechronstructive Potion for you all. It should be ready this afternoon. However, I do not think you should leave until evening because it was evening when you left home." She stood with her hands folded, looking very motherly. "You will have to go to bed as soon as you get there, no matter what time it is when you leave here. You want it to look like nothing unusual has happened so you will not have anything to explain to your parents, right?"

"That's probably a good plan," Martina agreed. "What do you guys want to do today?"

"Actually, if I may interject," Parisa said, "Alfwyn wanted to ask for your help in the office. He has a few things that need to be done, and he is a bit shorthanded with Malandros gone."

"That would be fun. Then we can talk to him about our ideas of where the Diana's Eye might be." London seemed to be excited about the plan.

"I'll let him know. Come down when you are ready for breakfast," Parisa replied. Then, she turned to leave the room.

"Hey Parisa," Martina said, "do you know why it's call the 'Diana's Eye'? Did it belong to someone named 'Diana'?"

"Oh," Parisa said. She tipped her head to the side and looked pensive. "Well, I know that it is supposed to be like the watchful eye of the goddess Diana, from Roman myth. She was the goddess of the moon, which is what keeps the tides in check. So basically, she is watching the moon to keep it in orbit, and the moon is tugging on the oceans.

"That's neat," Martina said.

"Sounds complicated," Heath said.

"I suppose it is," Parisa responded. She smiled and left the room.

After a moment of heavy silence, Heath whispered, "I don't know about you guys, but I'm excited to get some dirt on that sneak Malandros. I'm going to go through his desk. I bet I'll find all kinds of evidence to implicate him in the crime."

"Hopefully, we'll find something," Martina replied. "As long as he didn't take anything important with him when he disappeared, there might be some good stuff in there."

*   *   *   *   *   *

Later that day, after the trio had finished helping Alfwyn with the regular daily assignments, they sorted through what was left in Malandros's desk. As it turned out, Alfwyn didn't mind because he was also hoping that something would provide a clue about where Malandros was and what he was hiding. As they sorted through the papers, they perused every page for some small hint.

Martina heaved another stack out of the bottom drawer and shifted it to the floor. The worst part about trying to search the desk of a Rhihalva was that the drawers were charmed to be nearly endless. Rather than two or three regular-sized drawers full of papers, they sorted through a fathomless amount of papers in just one drawer. By mid-afternoon, they had not even begun on the other drawer in the desk.

Martina collapsed on the floor beside her stack and began to read. A few minutes later, she stretched her cramped limbs and rolled over onto her stomach, fighting the urge to clobber Heath for dozing off from boredom every few seconds. Looking at him, she realized it was more fun to watch him jerk back to life every time his head started to roll toward one of his shoulders. Staring back down at her paper, she put one hand under her chin and let the other plop on the floor. Quickly, she picked her hand up and grimaced at the sticky substance she had placed it in. Whatever it was, it glinted with a golden hue that was so faint she wouldn't have noticed it if her nose hadn't been just inches above it.

"I, um, think I found something, guys," Martina said. Her words startled Heath out of his sleep again and made London look up quickly. They crawled over to Martina's spot on the floor. She gestured toward the shiny splotches on the tile. "Does this look like anything to you guys?"

"It looks like snot," Heath said. "That means that not only was Malandros a bad Rhihalva, but he was also a nose-picker," he deduced. He paused dramatically and waited for Martina to proceed.

Before Martina could tell him just how much he was behaving like her brother, London cut her off. "I think this is the stuff that was on the floor at the theater. It's probably just soda."

"Maybe it's nothing, then." Martina rested her forehead on her arms wearily. She could feel the coldness of the tile floor through the paper that she had cautiously placed between her hands and the floor to avoid any more contact with the sticky liquid.

Suddenly, her hand grew very hot, almost to the point that it was burning. "Ouch," she said. Sitting up, she raised her hands from the paper and looked at them. The hand she had been resting her chin on looked fine, but the hand that had touched the sticky substance on the floor was inflamed. "Look at my hand," Martina cried. She could do nothing but stare at her hand as it began to swell.

London ran into the next room to tell Alfwyn what had happened.

"Oh, Great Garden of Afalonga. That cannot possibly be," Alfwyn exclaimed upon seeing Martina's hand and the sticky golden goo. "Do not touch any more of that. I will be right back."

As Alfwyn raced away, they watched in horror as Martina's hand developed white spots on the flaming red palm.

"It's burning and throbbing," Martina said. She stared worriedly at her hand, wincing from the pain.

Quickly, Alfwyn reappeared with a mortar and pestle, grinding away at a powder that glinted gold. Reaching into a pocket on his black tunic, he pulled out a corked tube full of a clear liquid. Allowing only a couple drops to fall into the mortar, Alfwyn continued to crush the powdery substance with the pestle until he formed an iridescent paste.

"Hurry," London said.

Finally, Alfwyn asked Martina to hold out her hand and, wearing a pair of thick leather gloves, he smeared a liberal amount across the affected area.

Almost instantly, the swelling decreased and the whitish areas, which were bulging ominously, went back down. Martina stared at her hand and flexed her fingers. Finally, she found her voice. "The pain is going away a little. What exactly is that stuff?"

"This is a mixture of powdered Unicorn horn and extremely purified water," Alfwyn explained. "It is so pure, in fact, that you cannot drink it because your digestive system can't tolerate such perfection. However, when you mix it with the Unicorn horn, it becomes a healing paste. Most general ailments can be cured with Unicorn horn. It is especially good for stomach aches." Alfwyn relaxed into the desk chair and propped up his injured leg on the open drawer.

"I meant, um, what is this stuff on the floor?" Martina prodded.

Removing the gloves, Alfwyn stared at the floor by Martina. "It is dreaming tree sap. I cannot imagine how it got here."

"We thought it was soda. Good thing we didn't eat it," Heath remarked.

"It's stuck on the floor, Heath," Martina said. "Though I suppose *you* might have licked the floor, so yes, it is a good thing." Martina and London laughed, while Heath pretended to be offended.

Alfwyn did not crack a smile, however. "Is that a shoeprint?" He leaned forward in his chair. "Do you see sap anywhere else?"

"I see a few sticky spots here and there, but mostly just around the desk," Martina replied.

Alfwyn walked back to the doorway that led to the office, and they followed him. They tracked the footprints all the way to the front door.

"At least this proves that we weren't the ones who ruined the dreaming trees," Heath said once they had reached the foyer. "If it was on our shoes, then the tracks would go up to our tower, but they don't. They lead to Malandros's desk."

"Heath, you could be a detective." London nodded to him.

"The Alvar must be notified immediately. Malandros must be found," Alfwyn said. "Not since before I took the office of Head Rhihalva has anything so vile and sinister happened."

"What could he possibly have to gain from destroying the dreaming trees?" Martina queried.

"Even stranger, why does it appear that the Sychateros are in on this, too?" a voice added.

Turning around, the group looked up at the balcony. Parisa was frowning.

"I thought you were in your office, love," Alfwyn said. "Did you hear what is going on?"

"Yes, and I cannot believe we ever trusted that Rhihalva," Parisa said. "To think that he was here with all of us, and we never suspected . . . Had I ever known any untrustworthy Rhihalven, I might have been more suspicious."

"No one could have known this would happen. It is no one's fault." Alfwyn began pacing. "I am sure the Alvar can handle finding him." He stopped and turned to them. "Dinner should be about ready. You should go wash up. I will join you shortly." Alfwyn quickly returned to his office, his brow furrowed.

After dinner, Martina, Heath, and London returned to the tower to retrieve their things. Closing the door behind her, Martina heard a noise like sandpaper brushing against wood. Quickly, she reopened the door to see what creature she might catch slipping into their room. Instead, she found that the furniture had all vanished. Sadly she turned back toward the stairs.

"The furniture is gone," she told the others. If they were going to return, why would the furniture disappear? They had not left for good, she hoped. Maybe it was just like the map: when someone left, the place they had been in disappeared. It sounded like a strange philosophical thought to Martina to believe that a place exists simply because someone existed in it.

The whole Branimir family was waiting for them by the front door. Haldor, Torvald, and Brantrod volunteered to walk with them to the Rhihalva Travel Agency to see them off. As they hugged everyone, Alfwyn reached into his pocket and pulled out what appeared to be a spongy, dove-grey stress ball.

"This is a messengeorb," Alfwyn said. "When you decide you are ready to return, just squeeze this tightly in your palm until it emits a soft white glow. Then, speak close to it." He held it to his lips. "When I receive your message, I will notify the Alvar that one of the exits will be opened shortly. That way, they will be expecting you rather than worrying that we are under attack." Chuckling, he held the orb out to Martina, who placed it carefully in an empty pocket of the book bag.

"And one more thing." Alfwyn picked up three corked vials from the table in the entrance hall. Handing one to each of them, he said, "This is the Dechronstructive Potion that you need to drink." Alfwyn smiled at them. "Safe journey," he said.

After drinking the purple, viscous liquid from the vials, which tasted strangely like cappuccino according to London, the group finally left.

The triplets lead the way back to Rhihalva Travel, talking excitedly of all the fun things they would do when Martina, Heath, and London returned. Saying goodbye at the entrance, Heath agreed with the triplets that he, too, hoped another puppet show was in the near future. He chuckled once they were on the other side of the door.

"Stop it, Heath. That's so mean," Martina hissed.

Just inside, the desk clerk directed them to the silver doors at the back of the room. Of the thirty or so doors in all shapes and colors that lined the back of the main room, that one would take them home. Upon walking through that door, they found themselves back in the room with the blue bobbing bubble lights. Their footsteps echoed as they crossed the room, this time with no one stopping them. They exited into the cavernous stairwell on the other side.

The rest of the trek back was also no trouble. They climbed up the stairs and quietly walked back through the ice cream machine into the shop and then into Martina's house. All three returned to the sleeping bags in the living room where the movie they had started what seemed like ages ago was still playing.

"And it is exactly 11:18," Heath commented, looking from the clock to his watch.

Surely no one in the house would have noticed their absence in the five minutes that the clock in the living room claimed they had been gone.

Almost as soon as they rearranged themselves in front of the TV, one of the stairs creaked loudly. Turning, they saw a small head peering at them over the railing.

Once he realized that he was spotted, Teagan walked down the last two stairs into the living room.

Martina rolled her eyes and made a motion to get up.

"Did you guys have ice cream?" Teagan asked. "I want ice cream, too. It's not fair if you get ice cream and I don't. I'm not a baby. Why do I have to go to bed and not have any fun?" He pouted as he crossed his arms and looked sternly at Martina.

Martina sighed, ready to explain that they were just checking to make sure she had taken out the trash earlier, when Heath stood up.

"Hey, just the little guy I was hoping to see," Heath said. "I have a business proposition for you." He patted his pockets. "Why don't we step into my office, Mr. Mackenzie?" Teagan followed Heath into the kitchen, and the two chatted for a few minutes.

"What is he doing?" London asked.

"I have no idea. I'm almost afraid to ask him," Martina said.

Soon, the two returned, looking pleased with themselves. Teagan grabbed the railing with one hand and held out the other to shake Heath's. "It's been nice doing business with you Mr. Heath." He pumped Heath's hand furiously.

"Same here, Mr. Mackenzie. See you tomorrow," Heath said. Then, just as suddenly as he had appeared, Teagan disappeared up the stairway. Moments later, they heard his bedroom door close.

"How did you do that?" Martina asked.

Heath returned to his sleeping bag. "Let's just say I know my clients better than anyone," he said. "However, I don't like to reveal my business dealings to the public."

*   *   *   *   *   *

The next afternoon, Martina was helping her mother and Aunt Cassie with Willoughby's Sundae Best again. When they hit a lull in the customers, Cassie wiped off her hands and came over to where Martina was refilling the straw dispenser.

"I had the strangest dream about you last night," Cassie said. "It was this summer, but you were just learning how to make all the treats. It's pretty strange. It was so warm and sticky in here that even inside with the air conditioning, the ice cream melted as soon as we pumped it out of the machine," Cassie paused.

"Ew."

"I know, right? A rather brusque woman *commanded* you to make her a large chocolate strawberry shake. As you began mixing, you were very careful, just like you always are, to mix it on a low speed to prevent splashing."

"Of course," Martina said. She was interested to know what happened next in the dream.

"As you approached the end of this seemingly endless mixing, a small house fly, which were in abundance in my dream, had the panache to splash-down in the frothy, amorphous mass. You continued to mix without noticing. Handing it to her, I looked on, with joy, at the expression on that irritating woman's face as she sucked a whole fly up through her straw and chomped it into minuscule pieces with her massive teeth. She rolled it around in her mouth with her giant, cow-like tongue. And finally, she pushed it toward her esophagus to slip into her stomach and become nutrients for her ample, fleshy body."

"Okay, you're grossing me out now."

Cassie chuckled. "But then, as the woman turned to look at me, I knew there was something very sinister about her. But I don't know what. I've never seen her before, and the dream never showed me anything sinister." Pausing again, Cassie took a swig from her water bottle.

"What did she look like?" Martina thought that perhaps she would know the woman.

"She was very short and rather sickly looking. She had a long dark green dress on with long sleeves, which was weird because it was so hot outside. And her hair was flat and stringy. She was kind of plain looking. Does she sound familiar?" Cassie finished.

"Not a bit," Martina said.

"It's a shame Mr. Willoughby isn't here. He was an excellent dream interpreter," Cassie said.

"Yeah," Martina said. She turned her head and bit her lip, pondering the significance of this dream. Her first instinct, after spending so much time in Sheardland was to picture a Rhihalva in that long dress. But she couldn't place the description as anyone she had met. A few minutes later, Martina took an order from a customer who wanted a large *chocolate strawberry shake*. Weird.

*   *   *   *   *   *

That evening, Martina, Heath, and London started on their mission by riding their bicycles to Diamond Lake, just a few blocks away. A lot of their classmates hung out there in the evenings to swim and play basketball or volleyball. Tons of parents brought their children to the playground by the lake, and many more people used the trail that encircled the lake. The trio, however, planned to look for a fish.

As she removed her helmet, Martina looked out across the water. It was a little daunting, especially since she wasn't sure where to begin.

London and Heath waited for her to say something.

"I suppose we should look around the lake first to see if we can find any clues." Martina felt a little intimidated by the fact that they were there based on a hunch she got from a dream, and not even a very specific hunch.

"I think we should look for some big webbed footprints, since that would show us where the Sycateros have been," Heath said.

Certain she looked ridiculous staring at the ground, Martina crept to the edge of the water and began walking slowly around the lake with her cohorts. Because most people stayed near the dock when they were swimming, the ground and weeds were not disturbed away from from the populated area. The three proceeded around the lake, looking for any signs that someone had been there recently.

Secretly, Martina thought it was a lost cause. The flooding in Asia had been going on for a couple of weeks. If the Diana's Eye had been missing that long, what would they be able to find that would show them where it had been? On top of that, they couldn't drain the lake to look for the fish, so they had to remain on the shore searching for clues. Martina sighed hopelessly.

"Whoa. I found something," Heath said. He pointed excitedly at the mud where he was squatting. Sure enough, there were webbed footprints.

"The Sycateros!" London whispered.

Martina could barely believe her eyes. "My dream must have been right."

Heath scooped up a handful of gravel. "Let's see what kind of fish are in this lake," he whispered. Tossing a few pebbles into the water, he immediately drew fish who must have assumed he was throwing food. "Here they come."

"But they all look normal," London said. "I don't see any magical fish."

"What if the fish does look normal?" Martina felt suddenly discouraged again. "How will we know which one it is?"

Without warning, a very angry duck came waddling down the bank to where they stood. She quacked at them, scolding them for being in her territory and proceeded to chase them off by flapping her wings and hissing irritably.

They ran.

Once the trio was far enough away, the duck settled herself on her nest and glared from afar.

"You know, *ducks* also have webbed feet," Martina said sarcastically.

"I guess we're ready for the backup plan," Heath said.

"I haven't gotten that far yet," Martina groaned.

*   *   *   *   *   *

The next evening, Martina, Heath, and London pretended to test out Heath's tent in Martina's backyard so they could "see if they stayed warm in it." But the weather wasn't all that warm. For early June, the nights were still cool. In reality, they needed to be in the backyard together so they could talk about where the Diana's Eye might have been hidden without being overheard.

"I know we are going to move," London was saying. "I don't know when or where. My parents don't want to put the new baby in Great-Granddad's room, and the house is just too small." Clearly, they had gotten distracted from the topic without having any fresh ideas of where to find the Eye.

"You can't move, though," Heath said. "Not after we've all gotten to be such good friends."

"I guess this just has to be our last adventure together," London answered. She looked upset.

The trio continued to chatter and sympathize with London about her impending move. Gradually the subject changed back to the Diana's Eye as they left the tent and Martina reviewed her dream with London and Heath.

They walked around the backyard.

". . . then I was walking back toward the lake and I woke up," Martina finished. "I know we were just there, but the fish has to be somewhere in Diamond Lake. I just know my dream was right."

"But fish don't stay in the same place," London said. "They swim around. And people fish in that lake. The fish we're looking for could be long gone by now." She sat down on a swing and gently swayed side to side.

"You're forgetting that this would have to be a magic fish" Heath reminded them. "That is, if the dream was directing us toward a fish at all."

"Martina?" Mom called from the back porch.

All three of them turned to look at her.

"You girls know the rules if you're going to stay out here. Make sure you stay near the house. It's getting dark." Mom set a bag of snack mix on the table and walked back in the house. "We're all going to bed soon, so don't stay up too late. I'll leave the back door unlocked."

Martina went to retrieve the snack mix and the three returned to the tent.

Inside, they nibbled and talked about the Diana's Eye some more. Soon, the house was in complete darkness.

"I'll be right back with some soda," Martina said. She stuck her head outside the tent, and the chilly air made her shiver.

As she crept along in the darkness—there's just something about darkness that makes you want to creep along—Martina nearly stepped on something that made her heart stop beating.

"What in the world?" she said.

Chapter 11 – Weather Makers and a Rhihalva from the Shadows

In the moonlight, Martina could barely see in what it was as she peered down. Quickly, she snatched the creature around the waist and held it up for Heath and London to see. It was barely eight inches tall and had sparse patches of blonde facial hair. Looking much like a tiny adolescent boy, the creature cowered in fear as Martina held him closer for a better look at him.

"Is he a Sock Gnome?" Heath approached them from the tent.

"I think so," Martina replied. "I wonder what he's doing outside of Sheardland," She hurried behind a tree where no one from the house could see the Sock Gnome. Heath and London followed.

"I am Noll, of the noble Sock Gnome Nation. Please, do not be angry," the Sock Gnome muttered. "The Head Rhihalva will be so upset if he finds out I was bothering the human children. We were curious about something particular that we learned from your socks."

He received stern looks from the humans.

"So you were after our socks again?" Heath said. "Why don't you buy your own or make them or whatever?"

"With all due respect, one cannot learn about your fascinating species from the socks that we make," Noll said.

"And what exactly have you learned about our species from our socks?" London asked.

"W-w-well, I, we have learned . . . that some of the females of your species wear their names on their socks," the Sock Gnome stuttered.

"We do?" Martina said.

"Yes," Noll said. "But usually, um, they are names like 'Angel' and 'Princess' and "Cheerleader.'"

"Those aren't names," London explained. "They are, I guess, characteristics? Maybe things that the girls want to be or are involved in?"

"I will have to report that to the commander," Noll said meekly. "May I please go so I can return to my home and be punished?"

"You think they will punish you for coming here?" Martina loosened her grip on him slightly.

"I was sent on a mission from the Sock Gnome Nation," Noll said. "I was supposed to regain the socks that were lost the other night. Just two of them though. Please do not be angry." He wailed as the three frowned at him.

"Why just two of them?" Heath asked.

"The ones with blue toes had a peculiar odor to them," the Sock Gnome stated. "We were wondering what we could learn from it."

Laughing, Heath said, "Those were my socks. And I'll tell you what you can learn from them. I was making a sandwich earlier that day, and I dropped some peanut butter on the floor and stepped in it. So, I guess my socks smelled like peanut butter and, well, stinky feet!" He shook his head and laughed.

"What is this 'peanut butter'?" the Sock Gnome asked.

"It's a food," Martina said. "You know, when we get back to Sheardland, we won't have a very good report either."

"Then why go back?" Noll queried.

"Because we also have to report a failed mission," Martina said. "We never found what we were looking for and have no evidence of how it was stolen."

"Maybe I can help," Noll said. "If you would be so kind as to give me something to take back, that is. You know, if I help you find what you need and you give me something I need, then we will both go back and be rewarded!"

"It's worth a try." London shrugged.

Martina nodded and placed the Sock Gnome back on the ground. "I'll be right back." Quickly she ran to her room and grabbed Aunt Cassie's green and black striped knee socks that she had given to Martina the Halloween she was a witch. Upon returning to the group and holding out her hand, she made her offer to the Sock Gnome. "You help us find what we need, and you get these. We don't get what we want, and you don't get what you want. Deal?"

The Sock Gnome eyed what Martina had brought. "Those are the biggest socks I've ever seen. The commander will be so pleased. Yes, it is a deal."

"It's an old pair of knee socks I've had for years," Martina whispered to Heath and London as they returned to the tent to discuss with the Sock Gnome what they were looking for. "It's a good thing I didn't throw them out."

"I never expected such a shrewd deal out of you, Martina," Heath said. "I've taught you well,"

Once inside the tent, they briefly explained to Noll about the Diana's Eye. Noll nodded in understanding. "Follow me." Picking through the wooded area in Martina's back yard, Noll led the group. He raced ahead of them to the bank of the stream and stopped near the edge of Martina's yard. Martina could just see him by the light of the moon.

"The milky sea . . ." Martina trailed off as she gestured to the stream. The bright swollen moon above reflected a bright white in the water, and the bleached, shallow bottom shone nearly white around it. Her companions smiled.

Jumping up and down excitedly, Noll pointed at the stream. "This is it! This is it! This is how they got in." He was standing by a point in the stream where it went entirely underground.

"How so?" Martina walked toward that part of the yard.

"This is a direct route into Sheardland." The Sock Gnome stopped jumping and looked puzzled. "They have to hold their breath a very long time for this though."

Martina, Heath, and London looked at each other. They all mouthed the same thing— "Sychateros."

Heath took a few steps away from the group. "Come look at this," Heath shouted.

They ran to the opening. In the shallow water near the rocks swam the strangest fish they had ever seen. It was swimming lazily back and forth and didn't seem to notice it was being watched. The fish was about a foot long and was covered in shimmery dark blue scales which faded through purple to pink at the tips of its fins. The most unusual thing about this fish was its eyes. One eye looked like a silvery cat's eye marble with a purple streak running through the center. When the fish blinked, the streak grew and shrank as it adjusted to the light. The other eye was completely missing, leaving a gaping black hole in its place.

"This has to be it," Martina exclaimed. She pulled her cell phone from her pocket and quickly snapped a picture of the strange fish.

"I guess your dream was right," London agreed.

"Thank you so much, Noll. This is all we needed to find." Martina started to hand him the socks.

"Wait a second," Heath interrupted. "Where exactly in Sheardland does this stream connect?"

"All the underground streams start at the Garden of Afalonga." Noll eagerly snatched at the socks.

Martina gave them to him and waved as he took off through the yard and disappeared from sight, no doubt toward a vent cover somewhere that was slightly askew.

"Are you guys up for a little ice cream?" Martina's sly smile said she didn't mean they would be eating any.

"Let's make like a banana," Heath answered.

London grinned.

Martina rolled her eyes and laughed.

*　　*　　*　　*　　*　　*

Once Martina, Heath, and London reentered Sheardland, the triplets met them at Rhihalva Travel, and they all returned to Adalborg. Because the sky had been cloudy for so many days and because of the recent chilly weather, the triplets brought heavy wool hooded capes for each of them.

On their way to the house, they met a group of Rhihalven talking in whispers near the end of the street. As they passed, they recognized Arist, the puppet-master and owner of Marvin's Magical Toys, among them.

The triplets smiled at him and waved.

With a flourish, he stepped out from the group and smiled broadly.

"Well, if it is not, now do not tell me, Torvald, Brantrod, and Haldor," Arist said. "Yes, of course. And how are your parents?" Before they could answer, he said, "Excellent. And these are your human guests. Forgive me if I do not remember your names. I have so much to remember with the toy shop." Arist babbled as he walked around them. His black cape swished with each movement, revealing his brilliant golden tunic beneath. "Allow me to introduce my wife and son to you. I do not believe you have met them. This is Uaithna and Svarok." He gestured to two members of the group who smiled forcefully and nodded in recognition.

The woman, who was rather short and pudgy, was clad in a dark emerald dress and matching cape which had been embroidered entirely in glittering threads. Her limp brown hair was pulled back from her chubby face a little too tightly by a bejeweled headband. Buried somewhere in the middle of all this skin was a pair of eyes like small smoldering lumps of coal.

The son was a tall, lanky athletic build with the same rugged good looks as his father and his mother's flat, limp hair. Svarok's deep pumpkin-colored tunic was flattering, but a large dark mole near the corner of his mouth was the most distracting feature about him.

Martina and London looked at each other and raised their eyebrows.

The other woman in the group had faded into the background. She wore a dress of mottled brown with a matching hat that shaded her face.

"I almost forgot," Arist said. "This is Lydia. She has an art shop just down the street." Arist stepped back so the diminutive woman could be seen properly.

She smirked at them and removed her hat with her short stubby fingers.

They stared at what the hat had been covering. Now revealed was a head full of greasy, unnaturally dark red, shaggy hair. Her sallow skin looked even sicklier than it had before with the revelation of this fiery mop. Smugly, she ran her stumpy finger through it to fluff it and blinked her large, dark brown eyes.

"It's nice to meet you all," Martina said. She tried to pull her gaze away from Lydia's hair. "We must be going, though. See you later."

As they started to walk away, Lydia called behind them, "Have a safe trip home!" Martina turned to look at the woman, and Lydia, Uaithna, Arist, and Svarok all returned her gaze while nodding or waving politely.

Inside the front door at the Branimirs', Martina, Heath, and London finally voiced their thoughts. "What was that supposed to mean?" London asked.

"That last comment was creepy if you ask me," Heath said.

"They were just being nice," Brantrod said. He picked up a ball from the floor and set it on the step beside the snapdragon, who was napping there.

"Yeah, Mr. Thanatolaus is very nice to us," Torvald added. "We always stop by the toy shop after school sometimes when Mom is at work. He lets us try out the new toys."

"Speaking of . . . check out our new piccah pipes," Haldor said. "We should play Pyra a song to show her how much we love her." He smiled as he pulled what looked like a small recorder out of his pocket. The other two boys followed suit, and soon, there was a discordant symphony in the front hall.

The snapdragon jolted from her nap and immediately ran to the corner of the room, disguising herself as a plant when she was as far away as possible.

Laughing, the group clambered up the stairway to the tower where Martina, Heath, and London were to stay again. At the top of the stairs, Martina looked back to find that Pyra was returning to the foot of the stairs to continue her nap.

Haldor clapped his hands together twice upon entering the empty bedroom, and instantly, the furniture that had been there before reappeared. "Let me know if you need anything else. See you later."

Just then, Alfwyn and Parisa entered the room. "I am glad to see you three again," Alfwyn said. He was carrying Ilona.

Parisa held a change of clothes for Martina, Heath, and London for the next morning. As she placed them on the dresser, she said, "I am happy you have returned. While you were back on the surface, did you learn anything that would help us find out where the eye might be?"

Martina briefed them on the fish with the empty eye socket and showed them the picture. They were more interested in how the mysterious camera phone worked, but she steered them back to the Diana's Eye and explained what Noll had said of the way the stream was connected to Sheardland.

Alfwyn stroked his beard and nodded. "That is interesting. Thank you for finding this out."

"You should make sure that you put on your capes any time you leave the house," Parisa said. "It has been unusually cold here today."

"That reminds me," Alfwyn began, "I wanted to offer to take you three with me tomorrow to see the weather Rhihalva."

"That would be great!" Martina replied instantly.

"I know how much you wanted that to be on the tour you took," Alfwyn continued, "and an opportunity has come up. The flood we just had in the Garden is making him so nervous about making it rain that he has had the rainclouds out for several days without letting them empty. I wanted to calm his fears in person." Alfwyn set Ilona down as she struggled in his arms. "I thought it would be a good opportunity to show you all his office."

Martina's friends agreed.

*   *   *   *   *   *

Early the next morning, Martina, Heath, and London were ready to visit the weather Rhihalva. After breakfast with the Branimirs, they met in Alfwyn's office and were surprised to see the triplets there too.

Alfwyn ushered them all into the side room with the glaislióir and wrote their destination on the pond. Then, they glaislied to the waiting room outside the weather Rhihalva's office.

Soon, they were walking into a large studio apartment. In one corner was the weather Rhihalva's living quarters, partitioned off with a curtain pulled back to reveal the cozy abode. Martina approved of the sky blue walls and the bed in the corner covered by a fluffy white comforter that reminded her of a cloud floating peacefully on a summer day.

The rest of the apartment was filled with charts and gadgets that the weather Rhihalva apparently used to design the weather in Sheardland. Big picture windows lined the apartment, affording views of most of Rhihalvberg from the hill that the apartment was perched on.

Glass cases lined one of the inner walls with a sign above denoting "Ancient Weather Equipment." Housed in the cases were large glass bottles full of liquid and pellets, a cone that was hollow except for a gelatin-like substance frothing at the bottom, and a series of globes with miniature models of the different lands in them.

Perched beside one of the large windows were a huge canvas and a palette with brushes. The canvas was covered with that evening's sunset, in shades of dull grey and blue. Sitting in the chair beside the window was the weather Rhihalva himself, gazing blankly toward the sky.

He turned when the group entered. He wore a tunic of the brightest yellow imaginable, trimmed in orange and red. "Hello, hello. I am Caelestis." His white shock of hair was thick and disheveled, but his grey eyes were still piercing. He shook Alfwyn's hand nervously.

While the rest of them looked around the office, Alfwyn talked to Caelestis about the recent flooding and the fears that Caelestis had about causing more flooding with the rain. Finally, they came to the agreement that, the next day, the rain would come in light showers to avoid another mess in the Garden of Afalonga. After assenting, Caelestis appeared much calmer and offered to show the group some of the instruments.

"The ancient Rhihalven made these when they first created Sheardland," Caelestis said. "They can be very destructive and were modeled after weather and natural phenomena that are present on the surface. Originally, they were created for defense, but have never been used. For example, during a rainstorm, there could be lightning, which could be created with this instrument here." He referred to a battered set of mirrors. "And this can be used to produce a whirl of wind known as a tornado." As Caelestis gestured toward the large glass bottle, something darted across the room and landed under the nearby table.

Quivering, he poked his round, bearded head out from under the table and stuttered, "Is-is there going to be a t-t-tornado?" His little hands both stroked the long, silky black beard so fast that it might be ripped from his chin.

"No, of course not, Hankin," Caelestis said. "I would never use this equipment. I was only telling them about it."

Martina knelt beside the table. "How do you know about tornadoes?" she asked the Sock Gnome.

"I used to travel to the surface as a representative of the Sock Gnome Nation to retrieve socks for research," Hankin began. This was greeted by skeptical "uh-huhs" from the humans. "And I had the misfortune of finding myself in a house where the humans were all awakened by a horrible siren somewhere outside. They all ran, startled and yelling about a tornado, to the basement. I did not know what to do, so I just watched." Hankin hung his head.

"What happened?" London asked.

"This swirling grey thing pointed out of the sky and ripped the trees out of the ground," Hankin said. "It threw things everywhere. I was so scared I came straight back home and never ventured to the surface again. I never wanted anything to do with our research after that. Luckily, Caelestis needed an assistant, and he took me in." He looked up at Caelestis admiringly.

"And your assistance has been invaluable, Hankin." Caelestis said.

Hankin beamed and then scuttled off to clean the paintbrushes and wipe up the paint splatters on the floor.

After dinner that night, Heath was hanging out in the triplets' room, teaching them some human card games and the concepts of winning and losing. Martina and London were lazing around their room discussing Malandros.

"This is the part I don't understand," Martina said. "The footprints clearly point to Malandros destroying the dreaming trees, but the puddles in the chemist's shop point to the Sychateros. But Sychateros are extinct. How does all this connect with the sleeping potion used to put the nymphs to sleep?" Martina pondered.

"No clue," London said. "And how did Malandros get the Diana's Eye so he could flood the garden, when the only way he could have gotten it without the Alvar knowing is by traveling through the stream in the Garden of Afalonga?" She frowned.

"There has to be a connection between the Sychateros and Malandros," Martina said. She leaned against the wall and pulled her knees in to her chest. "Alfwyn said something about Sychateros being aquatic creatures, right?"

"Definitely," London replied, "But how could they be aquatic and be able to get the sleeping potion from the chemist's shop?"

"Maybe Alfwyn would let us look at his books," Martina said. "We should go check." Martina and London left the room and ran into Heath in the entryway.

"Where are you guys going?" Heath said. "I have to tell you how I obliterated those three at Egyptian Ratscrew," he raved.

"Come on, we'll explain on the way," Martina replied. By the time they got to Alfwyn's office, they had told Heath everything. Telling Alfwyn that they were interested in learning more about some of the other creatures who lived in Sheardland, they were directed to the books they had looked at a few days ago. Finding the pages on Sychateros, Martina skimmed until she found what she needed.

"Here it is," Martina said. "'Sychateros are *semi*-aquatic creatures who have both lungs and gills.' I completely forgot. That's how they managed to stay underwater for so long, and then they could climb out of the water to steal the sleeping potion," Martina whispered.

"That still doesn't tell us where the Sychateros are now," Heath said. "Remember, they're supposed to be extinct."

"They would have to be hiding somewhere no one would go very often," Martina said.

"They would need easy access to the Garden to get to the stream," London added.

"I wonder . . ." Martina trailed off as she got up and strode across to the map of Sheardland. Looking over the map, she tried to figure out what would be the most likely place. Suddenly she stopped.

"What is it?" London asked.

"Hold on." Martina turned toward the Head Rhihalva. "Alfwyn, what streams flow into the stream that runs through the Garden of Afalonga, and what river does it flow into?" Martina hoped her question sounded innocent enough.

"Well, let's see." Alfwyn joined them at the map and pointed to the Garden. "All the underwater streams that cross the Earth's surface flow into that stream. Also, in Sheardland, a branch that flows right through Rhihalvberg empties into it. Then, it joins several other branches that flow into the Swamp of Sorrows. All of those branches empty into the Liadan River. Why do you ask?"

Martina smiled. "No reason. Just curious."

Later, the three were back in their room going over what they had learned in the book. "Exactly what I thought!" Martina said, piecing everything together. "The Swamp of Sorrows is the one place that no one goes very often. Remember, Chavdra said that Rhihalven only go there when they are sad. I bet that's where the Sychateros are hiding. Not to mention, it's close enough to the garden that they could probably slip in through the stream and travel through without being noticed. That way, they could easily steal the Diana's Eye."

"I just wonder what Malandros has to do with this whole thing," London said. "I can't figure out how he teamed up with the Sychateros."

"Do you think Malandros might have stolen the Diana's Eye from the Sychateros?" Heath said. "They stole it to flood Asia so they could have a new home, like someone suggested before. And then Malandros stole it from them to flood the garden so he could blame us and get us sent home. I wonder why he hates us so much?"

"It doesn't make any sense," London said. "Why *would* he hate us so much?"

"I think the only way we're going to find out is to actually uncover where the Sychateros are and see if they still have the Diana's Eye," Martina said. "Then, at least we'll know if they're working with Malandros. If they don't have the Eye anymore, then we know he stole it."

"Then let's go." Heath headed for the door. "We have to clear ourselves, and because the Alvar hasn't figured it out, it's up to us. We'll show those Elves how to sleuth."

"Heath, wait!" Martina rushed to keep Heath from being too rash. "We should talk to Alfwyn about this and see what he thinks. The three of us are no match for Malandros if we happen to meet him. Remember he's got magic!"

"Do you really think that Alfwyn is going to take this seriously?" Heath asked. "It has already taken so long for anyone to realize that Malandros might not be an honest Rhihalva that he could be long gone. These creatures, don't believe anyone can be bad." He threw his arms up in the air. "They have never met someone untrustworthy. Everything here is perfect. It's up to us to show them exactly what's going on."

"I agree," Martina said.

"And hopefully," Heath continued, "after we show them that there is a sinister plot to get rid of us, they'll improve their entertainment a little with some conflict. Geez." Heath stalked impatiently around the room.

Now that Martina had faced the result of all her clever deductions, she wasn't quite sure what to do. Her instincts told her that she should tell Alfwyn and let the Alvar take care of it. But, on the other hand, Heath was right. The Rhihalven would be very difficult to convince that something was amiss.

She swallowed and took a deep breath. "I think we should check out the Swamp of Sorrows and see if that's where the Sychateros are hiding. Do you guys want to try when everyone else is asleep?"

Heath and London nodded, Heath wearing a huge grin.

Martina smiled back apprehensively. What sort of weird expedition had she suggested they embark upon?

Chapter 12 - In the Swamp of Sorrows

Worried about their brightly colored clothes being spotted in the moonlight, Martina suggested they cover them with the black capes from the front hall closet. Quietly, they approached the front door, careful not to interrupt Pyra, who was sleeping stretched out across the bottom step to the towers.

Heath pulled a flashlight out of his book bag and followed the girls out the door. Martina glanced over at London, who didn't look the least bit scared. She wished that some of London's confidence would rub off on her. Swallowing hard, she stepped off the porch into the night.

Lights were out in all the shops they passed, and no one was on the streets. The entire town must have gone to bed. They passed the enormous Marvin's Magical Toys, with its colorful and enticing display window, and were soon walking down the winding lane toward the Garden of Afalonga once again.

Upon entering the garden, they were greeted by one of the nymphs, swinging nonchalantly in a hammock just inside the entrance in the dim light. As they approached her, she swung her legs over the side and glared. The trio dropped their hoods down and smiled at her.

"What do you think you are doing here?" she asked.

"We're helping to find Malandros and thought we would check out the stream," Martina replied.

"Why should I trust you?" the little nymph questioned.

"Because we helped Alfwyn clean up the garden and revive everyone after the flood," Heath said quickly.

"Good one," Martina thought.

The nymph circled, looking them up and down critically. Finally, she appeared satisfied. "Okay, I remember you. Hey, Flitterflower," the nymph called. Another nymph who had been napping in a nearby clump of daisies scratched her back and sat up. "You need to accompany these humans while they take a look around. And no more napping." She turned back to them. "I have never seen a nymph sleep so much."

"Sure thing, Shadowblink." Flitterflower continued yawning and stretching as she followed them through the sparkling dreaming trees. She watched them curiously as they followed the stream in the direction it flowed.

"Any idea how we can ditch our chaperone?" Heath whispered to Martina.

"I'm thinking," she replied.

Once they reached the rock wall, they had to climb the mountain to see where the stream came out on the other side. Luckily, this side of the mountain was not very steep, so they were soon at the top of the mountain and out of the garden. This is where the nymph left them and returned to her post—and probably her nap.

"That was easy," Martina thought.

Heath flicked off the flashlight.

Martina, Heath, and London waited until their eyes adjusted to the dim moonlight. They gazed in awe at the view all the way across an open plain in the distance. According to the map they had picked up from the lobby of the Rhihalva Hall of Knowledge, to the left was the Naidia Wood full of sleeping forest animals they had probably never heard of. And straight ahead, past the thick masses of vegetation, was Odhárna Fields where the giant wooly worms were also sleeping on their own wooly worm hair mattresses, unless of course they had been sheared. Far below them was a thick forest through which the stream ran a jagged path. At a point somewhere in the middle of the trees, the forest grew dense. Mosses hung from the canopy, along with tangled vines. This was where they needed to venture.

"Ah, the Swamp of Sorrows," Martina whispered.

"That it is," Heath said. He was pointing to the corresponding spot on the map.

"What now?" London responded.

"I guess we have to go in there and see if that's where the Sychateros are hiding," Martina said. "We certainly can't see anything from up here." Even in the dark, she could see London wrinkle her nose in disgust. "I know it's nasty, but we have no choice. If we want to know where they are, we have to start here."

"Why don't I just stay here and keep an eye out for anything unusual?" London asked.

Martina linked arms with her. "Because we have to stick together," she answered.

"Who knows if one of those crazy Rhihalven who didn't read the paper might be lurking around waiting for us to come back to the scene of the crime?" Heath said. He held onto the rocks as if he were ready to spring down into the middle of the swamp. This was what Heath liked best and Martina liked least: not knowing what was going to happen next.

The trio began their descent into the forest below, despite London's protests. The task was difficult due to the cleaving of the rock as they went. They seemed to bring down half the mountain with them as they crept along. Chunks of rock slipped off with every step and went skidding into the brush below.

"So much for sneaking in," Martina thought. She struggled to keep her balance on the sliding rocks and barely made it to the bottom without falling. As Heath skidded to a stop beside her, London took a step too far and tripped over a protruding root.

London's eyes welled up with tears. "Wow, that really hurts," she whispered through clenched teeth. Gingerly, she touched her ankle and winced.

Martina closed her eyes. Why did this have to happen to them now? "Do you want to sit for a minute and see if maybe then you can get up?"

"I, yeah, let's just wait a minute," London said.

The three sat in the silence of the swamp on a pile of rocks that had slid off the mountain. No one said a word as the minutes ticked by, and London maintained her position firmly on the ground. Finally, Martina knew they needed to at least try to go on.

"OK, London," Martina began. "Give me your arm, and I'll help you up."

London stared at the ground a moment and then finally offered her arm. Heath stood and wrapped his arm around her waist to give her extra support. Slowly, London stood. She placed her foot on the ground and started to put pressure on her foot.

"I think I'll be ok if we just walk slowly," London said.

"That's good," Martina responded. "I'm so relieved."

Quickly, they brushed the dirt from their clothes and stood quietly a moment to be sure that no one had heard them.

Heath flicked on the flashlight.

Finding the stream again, they began tracing it through the forest toward the swamp. In places, the thick maze of underbrush was so difficult to cut through that they nearly lost their trail. After what seemed like forever, though, the ground became soggier, eventually turning to a viscous muck that made walking nearly impossible.

London stopped and leaned against a tree, raising her injured foot off the ground. Barely audible, she breathed, "Now what are we going to do?"

Martina and Heath stopped, too.

Looking around her, Martina realized that she really had no idea. She almost expected to find a small Sychatero village or dwellings of some sort in the middle of the swamp. All they had found so far was what they already knew they would find: mushy ground and thick vegetation.

Nearby, a bubble rose to the surface and popped, releasing an eerie moan and sobbing. The whispers of past sorrows in the distance could be heard as if a wind were blowing steadily through the trees.

Now that they had stopped, Martina wished that they had never even returned to Sheardland. She would have been happy sleeping in the tent in her backyard at that point.

"I don't really know what to do now," Martina whispered. "I guess we should look around here for signs of life? I was expecting to see tree houses or something."

In the dim glow of the flashlight, Martina could see that her companions were as frightened by the swamp as she was. They all remained still, not wanting to venture off alone.

The ground sucked as Martina finally released one of her feet and turned away from the group. As she took her first slow step, the sound of cracking branches cut through the stillness. Even the lament from the past sorrows surfacing all over the swamp seemed to stop and listen. Martina's heart almost halted completely. She knew they were not alone.

Holding her breath, she supported herself against the nearest tree trunk and swiveled from the waist and neck to keep her feet from making the sucking sound. She peered off into the direction of the cracking branches and strained to see what might have made it.

The snapping echoed through the swamp again, this time, farther away. Martina strained to see what it was, trying to imagine what sort of creature could make such a horrible racket. Anything that could cause tree branches to break so violently had to be large.

She made eye contact with Heath who grinned and pointed in the direction of the sounds. He then pointed at himself and moved his arms like he was jogging. Martina shook her head "no." She was fairly certain that Heath had just offered to run after the creature and tackle it: a feat that would be challenging with the swampy ground.

London, however, was not moving a single part of her body, aside from her eyes, which were open wide in terror.

After hearing the third crash even further away, Heath pointed in the same direction again mouthing "Follow?"

Martina nodded skeptically and made a small motion to London to do the same thing.

London, however, jerked her head a tiny bit left and right to indicate that she did not plan on moving any time soon.

Heath left without looking back. Martina put her arm around London to help support her and started walking. Moving slowly to avoid loud slurping noises, the three approached the source of the noise cautiously. Suddenly, Heath stopped and held his hand up to keep them from running into him. In the dim light, they couldn't see why Heath had halted.

Again, the snap of breaking tree branches resounded in the darkness only a few feet ahead of them. As Martina watched through a gap in the trees, she could barely discern a figure bent over gathering a pile of branches together. It appeared to be of human form, walking upright, but it had a very broad torso. In the dim light, Martina couldn't distinguish its features.

Heath pointed and laughed silently.

Martina, shaking her head, could only assume that he was laughing at the creature's bare bulbous butt, which stuck up in the air awkwardly every time it bent to pick up its load. Once it had gathered all the branches, it staggered back toward the mountain.

The creature lumbered awkwardly through the dense brush. Its feet made loud thwapping sounds as it slapped each one down in the muck. Eventually, it reached the mountain that Martina, Heath, and London had just climbed down. With its cumbersome bundle, the creature began climbing a path that led diagonally across the mountain toward the side that faced away from Rhihalvberg. Then, just as suddenly as it had appeared, the creature disappeared around the side of the mountain.

For a moment, they all stared after the creature as if it might appear again. But it didn't.

"Should we follow it?" Martina asked half-heartedly.

"And the other option is what?" London eyed the stream that lead back into the safety of the garden.

"The other option is to go back to the Branimir's house," Heath said, "and wonder for the rest of our pathetic lives what that creature was and where he went. If you guys want to do that, then go ahead. I'm heading up that mountain." Heath crossed his arms and looked sternly at the girls.

Looking up the mountain, Martina swallowed hard. She had never liked heights, and this path ran up the side of the steep part of the mountain. Because she was pondering the possibility of falling off a mountain or being mauled by strange magical animals, she didn't want to be hasty in her decision.

"You guys go on without me," London said. She sat down on a log and stuck her injured foot straight out in front of her.

"London, we can't leave you here," Martina answered. "What if something happens to you?"

"But what if something happens up there?" London said. "How exactly would I help? It's better if I stay here."

"We can't go without you," Heath answered. "We've come this far together, as a team, and we have to finish this thing as a team."

London sighed. "Are you sure you don't mind going slowly because of me?"

"Of course not," Martina said. "You have to be there when we find out where the Sychateros live. So let's go, ok?" Martina held out her hand.

Finally, London nodded, giving her assent.

Heath swung around and placed a foot on the path. London put her arm around Martina's shoulders, and together, they followed him.

At first, the climb was easy. They followed an even path that wound halfway around the mountain. However, they soon found that the creature had a good reason for taking this route. If it had something to hide, no one would be able to follow the path unless they knew about it. At points, Martina wasn't sure they were still on the trail. Luckily, Heath had an uncanny sense of navigation. Despite the rocky outcroppings that obscured their footing and the patchy grass and weeds that made the path appear to be long unused, he always managed to spot broken branches or footprints that kept them on the trail.

As they wound their way up the mountain, Martina continuously kept her gaze up so she couldn't see how far away the forest floor was. Just when Martina was about to ask for a break, Heath stopped and gasped in awe.

"You guys have to see this!" He scuttled a little farther on the path.

As Martina got closer to where Heath stood, she could see what he had been so excited about. Everything beyond the mountain glowed an unearthly white. Even the reflection from the moonlight seemed to be swallowed by this flat whiteness.

"Is it . . . snow?" London asked.

"No, it doesn't snow here," Martina reminded her. "It must be the edge of their world. Remember what Alfwyn said about the map? How there is just nothing where no creatures are living? That must be it. It shows up as whiteness to us. Like the room they were having redecorated in the house."

"I wonder what it would be like to walk out there," Heath said. "Would I just smack into a wall of nothingness or could I venture out and make a place of my own where no one would be able to find me? Hey Martina, if I went out there, do you think anyone would be able to see me?"

"Let's not try it. You could get lost and never be heard from again," Martina said. "You don't know if you can even see Sheardland once you step into the whiteness."

Heath continued gazing for a moment and then proceeded along the path. Another fifteen minutes passed before they finally reached what appeared to be their destination. Just ahead, the ground formed a large, flat entryway to a cave.

Heath glanced around the corner. "The entrance is clear."

As they moved toward the opening, Martina could see a dim light shining from within the cave. She could make out some stray twigs lying on the ground. This must be where the creature brought the branches.

Taking a few more steps forward, but staying close to the wall, Martina was finally able to see the dazzling sight inside the cave. Near the entrance was a vast pond that stretched on into darkness. The surface glinted with a greenish light, the tint caused by the light reflecting off the green flecks in the stone walls. As some of the flecks moved, Martina realized that they were tiny insects. "Like lightning bugs, they're bioluminescent," she thought. It was her favorite word from science class that year.

The pond undulated, making little waves that lapped the edge of the rocky shore. To either side of the pond were corridors that wound off somewhere deep inside the mountain.

"Should we go in?" Martina wondered, however, what they were going to do if they actually found something.

Yet again, Heath was ready to explore. "Absolutely, I want to see what's down those halls. I bet that creature we saw went down one of them."

"Let's stick to the main room for now." London eyed the slime on the walls.

Careful not to make a sound, they crossed the threshold and entered the main room of the cave. Martina watched as the yellowish water swelled and then receded. Except it undulated more like Jell-o than water. It seemed thick. She got closer to the edge and found a sight she was *not* expecting.

Far below the surface, Martina saw large hulking shapes lying completely motionless on beds of branches. "This must be where that creature disappeared to," she whispered. There were a lot of them, filling the bottom of the pond, all apparently sleeping. They looked slimy with skin like grayish-green rotting flesh. The webbed footprints on the path were much larger than a duck's—Sychateros had webbed feet for swimming. The long slits along their necks, the gills, flapped open and closed freely as they breathed gently in their sleep. The skin was sunken in deep rifts all over their heads, like a close up of a gob of spaghetti. The ears were only a hole surrounded by fuzzy white hairs.

Martina shivered as she stared at the creatures. She felt relieved they hadn't gotten too close to the one they saw in the forest earlier.

Martina motioned for Heath and London to join her. For a minute, the three of them gazed down at the sleeping animals.

"They look like fish with feet," Heath said.

"Those have got to be Sychateros," Martina said. "I guess they aren't extinct."

"Looks like I was right," Heath said, beaming.

As Martina peered into the water, something deep in the pond caught her eye. Sitting on a pedestal made of rock was a ball in a transparent bag. It was round and silvery with a purple streak running through the middle. Its sheen was dulled through the bag, but it was still unmistakably Diana's Eye.

She pointed at the Eye and smiled excitedly.

Heath punched the air with his fists triumphantly. "Should we go after it?" he said.

"I don't see how we can," London began. "Those Sychateros are everywhere. Who knows what they would do if someone disturbed them. We don't know if they're violent or if they can see well in water. And maybe the pedestal is booby-trapped."

"I think we can rule out booby-traps on that pedestal," Martina said. "It's a pile of rocks. And, besides, no one even knows about this place, so no one would just stumble across it. It's too perfectly hidden."

"And don't forget," Heath said, "we have one of the best swimmers in the world with us." He patted London on the back.

"Um, I don't know where you heard that." London gave Martina a bewildered look. "I'm on the *middle school* swim team, not the *Olympic* team. I can do pretty well against middle school *humans*. I don't know how I'd do racing something that actually lives in the water." London frowned and glared at the depths. "Besides, I can't swim in that. What if they pee in the water? It's all dirty and gross. I don't even have my goggles. And my foot hurts."

Martina frowned. There was no way she could swim down there. She was slow and couldn't hold her breath long. The thought of being grabbed by the slimy aquatic creatures made her shudder. "So, I guess we should climb back down and tell Alfwyn that we know where the Eye is. Then the Alvar can retrieve it."

"That's fine with me." London seemed satisfied. "I'd prefer that to swimming in the nasty Sychateros' water."

Martina was glad to hear her say that.

"If you want to go back, you can, but I plan on getting the Diana's Eye back no matter what," Heath said. He puffed up his chest and eyed the Sychateros, apparently ready to fight.

London looked into the water again. She touched it with her fingertips and quickly removed them rubbing them together. "It doesn't feel *that* nasty. It's actually warm." She took a couple deep breaths. "I guess I could try. The water doesn't look too deep. I can definitely hold my breath that long."

London peeled off her cape and shoes and brushed her hair back from her face. She walked over the ground with her feet curled up to avoid as much contact as she could with the cold dirt. Finally, she reached a point where she was close to the Diana's Eye but far enough away from most of the Sychateros that she could lower herself in.

Martina and Heath watched London swimming across the surface of the pond toward the pedestal as her gown billowed out behind her.

Some of the Sychateros stirred but did not wake up.

Martina hardly dared to breathe. If something did happen while London was in the water, Martina wasn't sure what she could do. She had never been more nervous in her life than she was as she watched London retrieving that Eye.

As she hovered above the Eye in the water, London turned back to look at Martina and Heath. Then, she swam back to them. "I'm sorry. I just can't do it. It's really bothering my ankle to swim, and I won't be able to get enough power to go clear to the bottom."

Heath helped pull London out of the pond and wrapped her cloak around her to dry her off.

Martina frowned. Now what? As she watched Heath comforting London, she knew what she had to do. "Guys, I'll get it." She peeled off her cloak and twisted her hair into a knot at the nape of her neck.

"Are you sure about that?" London asked.

"Of course she's sure," Heath answered. "Mr. Willoughby would be proud."

He had to drag Mr. Willoughby into it. "Right, here I go," Martina said. She gazed down into the gel-like water and quickly climbed in. It was hard to move through, but somehow she was soon treading water above the pedestal.

Martina made a skeptical face to which Heath responded with an energetic thumbs-up. Martina nodded slowly in agreement. Taking a deep breath, she plunged beneath the surface and pulled herself quickly to the bottom. She reached for the Diana's Eye, while the bag it was in rose and fell in the water. Grasping it, she yanked it from the pedestal and paused, as if expecting an alarm. She jerked her head toward the sleeping Sychateros.

With the Eye in her hand, Martina pushed off from the bottom and shot to the surface. Heath pulled her out of the pool and wrapped her cape around her.

As Martina swam to the surface, however, her vibrations from pushing off so hard woke one of the Sychateros that was sleeping near the Eye. He rubbed his gelatinous eyes and looked around

As the first Sychatero started rousing the others and pointing at the empty pedestal, Martina jumped into her shoes, tucked the Eye, still in its bag, inside her soppy cloak, and sprinted for the entrance to the cave. Heath helped London up, and the two darted after her, London limping the whole way.

While they ran to the entrance, Martina saw the Sychateros sloshing violently around their pond searching for the Eye. She dashed out of the cave and started down the rocky path.

If the climb up had been difficult, the descent was even more so. In the dark, they tripped in their haste over rocks and dropped tree branches that they had easily stepped over before. Eventually, they made it back to the ground and were skirting the edge of the mountain when they heard something and looked up horrified. Sliding down the mountain path was what appeared to be a clear greenish-yellow river. It frothed and foamed as it moved, lifelike, down the mountain, disregarding any obstacle in its path.

Chapter 13 - Marvin's Magical Toys

"Run!" Martina screamed.

"I can't," London said. Tears streamed down her face as she limped and hopped trying to keep up with them.

Heath bent his knees and reached behind him. "Hop on!" he said. "You can't weigh much more than a tuba."

London hesitated.

"Just do it," Martina said. "We don't have time to think about it." She grabbed London's arm and helped her onto Heath's back.

The three took off as fast as they could back toward the town. If sloshing through the thick, marshy swamp was difficult before, running through it now was impossible. Using the trees like stationary ski poles, the group pulled their way through the swamp as best they could.

The precious time they lost in the swamp allowed the Sychateros to gain on them, swimming in the stream they brought down the mountain with them. Their webbed feet and moist skin helped them to cut through the mud easily, covering ground much faster than Martina, Heath, and London could. At the edge of the swamp, Martina made one final push from the trees, and snagged her cloak. Ripping it from the branch, she barely got away before one of the Sychateros snatched at her with his long, gnarled fingers, gargling something menacing at her.

Rounding the mountain, the trio was finally able to speed up. As they quickened their pace on the firmer ground, they managed to get a little ahead of the Sychateros, who could not move as quickly on the grass and road that led toward the bridge. Here, webbed feet were definitely a disadvantage, like running in flippers.

Martina, Heath, and London passed the entrance to the Garden of Afalonga but continued toward Rhihalvberg with the hopes of outrunning the splashing water behind them. Rounding a corner in the path they were following, Martina glanced back. Angry arms and webbed feet flopped from the amorphous mass. The stream was full of violently angry Sychateros. "They must be able to create a stream around them so they can travel faster. Maybe that's how they broke into the chemist's shop," Martina called to Heath and London. Heath grunted in response.

Thundering across the bridge, Martina could see the outline of the town looming ahead of them. Something felt vaguely familiar about this. First running from dragons, now Sychateros.

The longer they ran, the more the stream seemed to gain momentum, and the slower Heath ran with London on his back. The stream was like a waterfall. The Sychateros were able to gain on them traveling in their stream, closing the gap and crossing the bridge not long after. Like sharks attacking a school of fish, they gnashed their talon-like teeth and charged. A gurgled command could be heard muffled by the water after they reached the open field beyond the bridge, and they spread their forces out, preparing to encircle the trio as they closed in.

Finally, the humans made it to the edge of the town. "We couldn't outrun the snapdragons, so we probably won't be able to lose the Sychateros," Martina said. "And Heath will fall over if we keep up this pace much longer," she thought. She racked her brain for some other plan, her legs throbbing painfully. Her breathing grated against the constricted passages in her throat as she rushed for the nearest door. She turned the handle, and it was unlocked. "In here!" she screamed. Jerking it open, Martina, Heath, and London rushed through the front door of Marvin's Magical Toys and slammed it behind them.

The water slowed as it approached the door ominously.

They shoved the heavy wooden checkout counter against the door, hoping that the Sychateros couldn't squeeze through the crack underneath or use their strength to break down the door.

"It amazes me that the Rhihalven don't lock their doors," Heath said. "They must trust everybody."

Martina peered through the display windows by the door at the puddles of water which had surrounded the building.

An eerie silence enveloped the trio standing in the dark with only the light of the streetlamps shining menacingly through the windows, causing an orange glow and long shadows within the shop.

Outside, the Sychateros treaded water in groups in their puddles, probably planning for the perfect moment to attack. The trio couldn't stay inside the shop forever, and the Sychateros certainly knew that.

Martina slumped against the desk. "There has to be some way to get rid of them."

London started sobbing. "We are never getting out of here. I just know it."

Martina hugged her. "We'll get out. I swear. But we all have to look for a way, so come on." She smiled at London.

"You have to stop crying," Heath said. "When I see someone cry, I start crying. And we don't want to leave Martina to take care of us while we bawl our eyes out, do we?"

"I'm okay." London sniffed. "Maybe there's some sawdust stuff here somewhere," London suggested.

"Ash of Death?" Martina asked. "What are the chances of that?"

"We should at least look," Heath said. "We have to return the Diana's Eye to Alfwyn."

The three of them dug through the desk drawers, which were, thankfully, *not* enchanted like Malandros's desk.

"And nothing," Martina said. "Why didn't I read more about the Sychateros? I remember reading that they have lungs and gills and that they have terrible eyesight."

"Then how could they follow us so closely?" London asked.

"They sense movement, remember?" Heath said. "That's how they find food."

"Ugh. Let's just try to find something to distract them with," Martina said.

"There has to be something around here," Heath said.

"Or maybe they have some Ash of Death in this box of junk by the door," Martina said. As she dug through the box, she bumped into something with her foot that set off a strange wooden clanking that echoed eerily in the shop. Finally able to see, now that her eyes had adjusted to the dark, she had to bite her lip to keep from screaming. She found herself face to face with one of the life-sized puppets from the puppet show they had seen. She backed away and turned to the others.

"I think I have something," Martina whispered. "Do you think we could get the Sychateros to believe that some of these puppets are us?" she asked.

"We could try," Heath said. "Then we could escape when they capture the puppets." Heath touched one of the lifeless marionettes.

"I thought these were creepy the night of the puppet show," London said. "Now that they aren't moving, they're terrifying."

"Well, *we* are pretty terrifying," Heath said. "I'm sure the Sychateros will think these are us."

"So, how did the Sychateros wind up with the Diana's Eye?" London asked. She sorted through the puppets trying to find one that looked like her.

"Who knows?" Martina said. "Someone had to put them up to it, though, since they don't come up with ideas on their own."

"But no one knows they exist except us," London said.

"We can figure that out later," Heath said. "Let's pick out some puppets and get out of here." He brushed some dust from the front of a curly-haired puppet. The likeness to Heath was remarkable. He lifted it from the hook and held it up beside him. "How's this one?"

"He's your twin." London glanced from puppet to Heath.

Soon, Martina and London had also found marionettes that resembled them and pulled them down from the hangers. "I know Sychateros don't see well, but I would feel more comfortable if the puppets wore our capes." She took off her own and wrapped it around her avatar. "The problem now is how to make them move outside while we are in here," Martina said.

"We can use these poles to stick them out the door," Heath said. "Hopefully the Sychateros will grab them right away." Heath grabbed a few long wooden walking sticks that were leaning against the corner behind the door.

Martina, Heath, and London worked on the puppets for the next few minutes. They ran the poles under the arms of the puppets and through their sleeves so they could hold each of the puppets up while they thrust them out the door.

The Sychateros shifted and paced across the front of the shop.

Martina wiped sweat from her forehead. If they got themselves out of this one, it would be an amazing feat, she thought. She was concentrating so hard on the task at hand that she hadn't heard the footsteps on the balcony above their heads.

"Look what I found!" echoed a gruff voice from above. "Three little blind mice. Would you like me to turn on a light for you?"

They looked up, startled. Heath grasped one of the walking sticks in his hand and stood up. "Who are you?" he demanded.

"I might just as easily be asking you the same question," the voice replied. "Who exactly are you? What are you doing wandering around in here in the middle of the night? That's very risky behavior for those who do not know the dangers of the land they are in. Especially for those who *do not belong here*." The hollow staccato of fingers tapping on a railing echoed through the shop.

"Malandros?" Martina whispered.

London squinted and leaned forward. Heath stayed a few steps away from the girls, still gripping the stick, ready to swing.

"I know you think you have learned so much while you have been down here," the voice continued. "You may think you know so much more than Rhihalven, but did you learn, perhaps, that wild snapdragons have a particular thirst for little mice such as yourselves?"

As Malandros finished speaking, Martina could hear a slow and steady scuffing sound. As she peered into the darkness on the main floor, she thought she saw something move. What little bit of light there was glinted off something that had shifted at the back of the shop.

A sudden popping noise echoed through the building, and Heath braced himself, looking around wildly as Martina and London jumped to their feet. They knew exactly what that noise meant, but the exact location of the snapdragons was too difficult to tell in the dark.

"I almost forgot the lights," Malandros said. "How else am I going to 'see how you run'?" his voice boomed as light flooded the entire store and workshop.

Toward the back, Martina could see clusters of flowers, oddly enough, sprouting out of the floor. At that moment, the snapdragons appeared to be dormant, but Martina knew they wouldn't remain that way for long. Grabbing Heath and London, she did the first thing that came to her mind. She ran for the stairs to the second floor. Maybe, if they were lucky, the snapdragons wouldn't be able to climb the slippery metal industrial stairs.

When they were about halfway to the stairs, the snapdragons sprang to life. Snapping after them, the frightening flowers chased them to the foot of the stairs. Martina and Heath were able to climb with relative ease due to the rubbery soles of their shoes. They pulled London up the stairs with them and dodged around a huge tank of water full of squishy colorful balls.

The stairway slowed the progress of the snapdragons as they slipped and slithered, but it by no means stopped them. Snarling and spitting fire, the little dragons climbed the stairs, hungrily tracking their prey.

"How do you propose to get yourselves out of this mess?" Malandros's voice echoed from across the balcony. "Funny how you are here to destroy our world, and yet, it will destroy you," The trio could now see his unkempt hair and protruding belly.

"But we aren't here to destroy your world!" Martina screamed. "What could we possibly gain from that?" She tried to think of something to do.

"Wait a second, I've got an idea." Heath dug furiously in his pockets. As he did so, he jogged across to the wall where an assortment of colorful rubber hoses and other random things were dangling from hooks. Grabbing one of the hoses and finally wrenching his hand from his pocket, he crammed his tuba mouthpiece into one end of the hose. Placing the mouthpiece on his lips, he blew as hard as he could into the makeshift horn and swung the other end of the hose above his head.

The horrifying noise caused the snapdragons to panic, just as Pyra had done when the triplets made noise at the Head Rhihalva's house. They instantly ran as far from the source of the noise as possible, back down the stairs, sliding and falling over each other. Running down the hallway to the offices, they echoed frightened shrieks the whole way to the back of the building where they hid in a dark corner disguised as flowering plants.

"Quite clever, human," Malandros boomed. "Maybe you have learned a few tricks. Unfortunately for you, noise does not scare me away." He took a menacing step toward the group. Raising his hand, he uttered, "Cuman." Instantly, the keys that had been resting around their necks flew over their heads and directly into Malandros's grasp. He clutched them and glared at the humans. A smile spread over his face, revealing dirty yellow teeth behind his cracked lips. Taking a deep breath, he fingered the keys, looking for one in particular.

Martina, Heath, and London remained motionless across the balcony, unsure of what their next move should be.

"What's so important about those keys?" London asked bravely. "We only have them because we can't use magic. But you have magic and don't need the elements of water, fire, and air to fight us."

"Ah, but apparently Alfwyn did not tell you everything," Malandros replied. He dangled one of the keys from its strap and gazed at it. "You do not have a clue why keys such as these would be made, do you?"

The three stared at him. Martina hoped he would babble on about the keys, leaving her time to think of a plan.

"I did not think so." Malandros spit the words out. "You see, so many precautions have been made to keep the Rhihalven from ever having too much power. Yes, we have magic, but no Rhihalva has the ability to control fire, water, or air. That, too, was taken away from us when we were forced into hiding, taken away from us, *from the mighty Rhihalven*, and put, full force, into these three keys. Flooding could only happen if someone has the water key, or, well, the Diana's Eye."

Again, they said nothing.

"Fools," Malandros said, "only the one who holds these keys can possibly exercise power over these elements. Our magic has been decreased so much since the elemental laws and the keys came into existence." He clutched the keys to his chest. "And that horrible human, Artemidoros Willoughby was given them to protect from anyone who should desire their power." He glanced at the humans. "I guess he chose his successors poorly, did he not?" As suddenly as he had grabbed the keys, he held one in the air and shouted, "Debraeth."

Martina's quick reflexes kicked in, and she ducked before the spell hit her. But Heath and London weren't so lucky. Both of them were slammed into the wall and left gasping for breath. They panted, clutching their chests. Martina crawled to them, her heart pounding as she hoped that they were all right.

"Not bad. Not bad at all," Malandros said. He looked adoringly at the keys. "I am glad I studied the old powerful words that control elemental magic. It feels so good to speak them—like I am releasing them from thousands of years of lying in wait, rotting," Malandros cooed. He held up the key which was marked "Air." "Of course, I know many stronger spells I could put to use. I only knocked the wind out of you." He jerked his hand in the direction of Heath and London.

Martina jumped.

Malandros began inching toward Martina along the balcony. His eyes bored through her. The huge tank full of water along the wall reflected his form eerily in the glass. "By default, you would be the lucky one who gets to go first." Again, he smiled his sneering, maniacal grin.

Martina looked around her but could find nothing to stall for time or to fight against someone who could use magic and control the elements. She decided that trying to distract him would be the best plan. "What good will it do you to get rid of us?" She inched back a bit. "Even if we did want to destroy Sheardland, don't you think other humans would be ready to pick up where we leave off? Do you really think three kids would be stupid enough to take on all the Rhihalven?"

"Ha-ha-ha-ha-ha." His laugh was deep and throaty. "You do not really expect an honest answer to that last one do you?" He leaned back against the fish tank. "Of course I think you are stupid. But I must destroy you because then the Rhihalven would be safe from human invasion, because no other humans could access our land without knowing where the portholes are."

"But why fight us now?" Martina asked. "Let us go so we can get reinforcements. Then you can have a *real* battle. Wouldn't you prefer to take out your hatred of humans on all of us?"

"You really think this is all about you?" As Malandros spoke, sweat dripped from the end of his nose. "You did ruin our plans with the dreaming trees, but surely you do not think the whole idea is to simply get rid of you." Malandros grinned and tossed the keys back and forth in his hands.

"So you *did* try to destroy the dreaming trees," Martina pointed at him.

"In no way did I try to destroy them," Malandros taunted. "That's merely a consequence of our quest to make the Rhihalven aware of their situation." He leisurely dangled the keys from one hand swinging them gently back and forth.

"What situation?" Martina demanded. She glanced at Heath and London who were still breathless on the floor.

"Do I really have to spell it out to you?" Malandros feigned exasperation but was obviously pleased to reveal his brilliant plan. "The Rhihalven are being oppressed, and they do not even realize it. For 40,000 years, we have lived in this, this *hole*. We should be free to roam the Earth, not stuck here," he stomped his heavy boot on a loose floorboard, "playing babysitter to some inferior species. We had to let the Rhihalven know that humans caused us to trap ourselves here. The only way to do that was to flood the Garden of Afalonga with water from the Swamp of Sorrows." He touched the tank of water and made a whooshing gesture with his arms. "We called up the old memories of the battles with humans from the time before Sheardland. Then we used the Diana's Eye to flood the garden. With the sorrows from the Swamp in the Garden, we merely waited for the Rhihalven to go to sleep to start dreaming their replacement dreams."

Martina gasped.

"Of course, that is where you came in." Malandros glared intensely at Martina. "You figured out that something had to be wrong with the garden, and then you brought Alfwyn into it . . ."

"But what about the Sychateros?" Martina said. "Alfwyn said that everyone thought they were extinct." She was having trouble thinking of what to do while she tried to distract Malandros.

"Ah, not exactly extinct," Malandros said. "A small group of them have been living in the Swamp of Sorrows for the past forty years. Our great leader found them and recruited them for our cause."

"Great leader?" Martina thought.

"He told them that they could move to the surface soon," Malandros explained, "to a new place that they would flood, if they only retrieved a special little orb for us. The Sychateros recovered the Diana's Eye from the stream on the surface and took care of the nymphs for us." He crossed his arms. "Sychateros are quite useful once you have persuaded them of what they need to do. They can travel so easily, unnoticed, when they want to," he gloated. "But enough talk. Now is the time to finish my job."

"But what will you do once the Rhihalven are convinced they are being oppressed?" Martina blurted out. She had to think of something fast. Moving her foot back, she bumped into Heath's leg. He kicked her in response.

"That will have to remain a surprise, will it not?" he replied with a grating laugh.

"And how did the Sychateros know where the Diana's Eye was if no one else even knew it existed?"

Martina needed to think faster. Stalling was not working as well as she'd hoped.

"There is a wise, old sage living in the middle of nowhere who needed a little *persuasion* to talk." Malandros laughed and rubbed his palms together while still holding the straps of the keys. They jangled. "But she finally did. Ah, the question is which element I should choose to help me now." He fingered the keys, eyebrows furrowed in concentration.

Heath kicked Martina again, and she turned to give him a dirty look. Both he and London were regaining their breath. Heath motioned slightly to what he gripped in his hand. Then he gestured toward Malandros.

Martina nodded, knowing exactly what Heath wanted her to do. She clutched the bag with the Diana's Eye from Heath's outstretched hand while Malandros was still indulging his own reverie.

"I think that fire would be a bit too final for my taste," Malandros muttered. "Perhaps we should try water next?" With that, he held the water key out in front of him and met Martina's gaze.

"Absolutely," she replied. She ran to the opposite side of the balcony from where Malandros stood, hoping he would place so much faith in his magic that he would not follow her. As she did so, she tucked the Diana's Eye out of sight in her own pocket.

"'Run, run, as fast as you can.' Is that not what you ridiculous humans say?" Malandros asked. Then he laughed. "*I* can catch you. Even from here."

Again, he held up his hand with the water key and looked directly at Martina.

Before Malandros could say anything, Martina whipped the Diana's Eye from its protective bag and held it out directly in front of her, hoping desperately that it would work.

The water in the fish tank behind Malandros burst the side of the tank closest to the Diana's Eye in its rush to meet with the moon, on which the stone had begun to gently tug.

Struggling to maintain composure, Malandros thrust the keys up in the air and attempted to speak the words that would control the water. Caught completely by surprise and inundated by the water that sloshed down his throat, he sputtered, dropped the keys, and cracked his head against the metal railing. The mighty stream of water washed Malandros's fleshy form right over the railing, causing him to hit the hard floor one story below. Not another sound came from him.

As she slipped the Eye back into the bag, Martina felt relieved. She watched as the water and colorful balls sloshed over the railing and to the floor of the toy factory. Then, she peered over the railing at Malandros's limp form. He had become a soggy, lifeless, mangled heap—his fuzzy, abundant hair finally flattened by the force of the element he had tried to control.

When she was certain that Malandros was no longer a threat, Martina hurried back over to where Heath and London were. They were apparently still exhausted from their attack.

"Are you guys okay?" Martina asked.

"Yeah," London said, but she still looked shaky.

"Pretty much." Heath looked expectantly at Martina.

"What's wrong?" she asked him.

"I can't believe that you agreed with Malandros that he should use water against us," Heath said. "It would have sounded better if you'd said, 'You're threatening me with water? I'm *made* of water,' or something like that." He grinned. "I think that's how we should tell the story."

"Oh, no," London said. She clutched her stomach where the spell had hit her. "We still have to get out of here and past the Sychateros."

"And we have to tell Alfwyn that we defeated Malandros," Heath said. He struggled to get up too. "I mean, tell Alfwyn that *Martina* defeated Malandros."

"How are we going to get out?" London said. "I bet those Sychateros are still waiting for us."

Martina put her arm around London to help her walk, and the three of them descended the metal grated stairway to the now soggy main floor. As Martina stooped to pick up the keys near Malandros's purple crumpled body, she thought she would try one last resource. "Heath, what else do you have in your pockets?"

Heath grinned again and dug deep into his pockets. Dumping everything out on the big bay windowsill at the front of the shop, they examined his treasures. He had his tuba mouthpiece, a flashlight, some string, three pennies, two squashed Bug Bite candies, and a snowglobe containing a miniature version of Rhihalvberg.

Martina picked up the snowglobe and instantly recognized it. She frowned at Heath and then looked back at the snowglobe.

"I forgot about that," he said. Leaning in close to Martina, he explained, "I didn't want London to see me looking at a silly snowglobe, so I slipped it into my pocket when she came over to look at the ancient weather machinery. I forgot to put it back before we left the weather Rhihalva's house, sorry." He shoved both hands into his pockets this time.

Martina shook her head and smiled sympathetically. "Nevermind. I have an idea." She headed to the window and looked out. Through the dim light of early morning, she could barely make out the forms of the Sychateros below, thrashing impatiently in their sloshing puddles. The cloudy sky reflected a steely grey off the water in the street.

"You're not going to make it snow are you?" London asked. "What good would that do?"

"Maybe they'll leave because they're too cold," Heath added. "I'm sure they'd have trouble staying warm, being naked and all."

"That's not what I'm going for, though," Martina said. Flipping the snowglobe upside-down, she shook it.

"Nothing happened," Heath said.

Then, looking closely at the base, she saw a keyhole. Written in tiny letters above it, she read aloud, "Clouds may come and wind may blow, but without Water there is no snow."

Taking the water key from the table, Martina inserted it in the hole on the snowglobe's base. When the key handle grew warm, she knew she was on the right track. She wound the key and then turned the snowglobe over, shaking it hard several times.

Across the hills, she saw it first. The clouds grew thicker and darker. The flecks of snow began falling and moved swiftly across the deserted streets of Rhihalvberg. Swirling in the light breeze, the flakes tumbled toward the ground where the Sychateros lay unaware in their puddles. Soon the rooftops were coated like powdered-sugar doughnuts, and the streets were white with the fluffy crystals. In the snowglobe, the storm continued spinning dizzily over the tiny Rhihalvberg just as it did outside.

A shiver ran down Martina's spine. Gazing into the street, they could see that the Sychateros were in a peculiar predicament. Because the sun had not shown for several days, and because Sheardland was inside the Earth, the ground had grown very cold. Each of their puddles had frozen over from the contact of the snow and the cold ground.

When all the Sychateros appeared to be frozen immobile, Martina opened the front door and ventured outside with Heath and London. They slipped and slushed their way down the street toward Adalborg. Some of the Rhihalven peeked out of the windows and doors, obviously marveling at the strange white stuff falling from the sky. They clapped their hands, excited by the fluffy gift from above.

"Not to worry, brave Rhihalven," Heath exclaimed unexpectedly. "You are all safe now. No need to thank us."

"Shhhh," Martina elbowed him.

The Rhihalven were reacting very strangely, pointing at the sky and catching snowflakes in their hands to examine them. Martina didn't want to draw too much attention in case someone decided that snow was dangerous and they were the cause.

Once they reached the house, Alfwyn greeted them at the front door. "I couldn't sleep," he explained. "I felt that something great was happening but could not place what it was. When I found your beds empty, I assumed you were the cause and came down to wait for you. Do you have an explanation?"

As the trio recited their story, Alfwyn nodded and stroked his beard. He soothed London's ankle with unicorn horn paste as they spoke.

"I wish you had waited for my help," he said, "but I am glad to see that you have come out of it so well. And the snow," he winked at Heath, "is a lovely touch. I will alert the reporters immediately. The front page will announce how Malandros reached his soggy end, why the Sychateros are ice statues in front of Marvin's Magical Toys, and, of course, what *snow* is!"

Martina smiled tiredly at Heath, London, and Alfwyn. It had been a long night, and she could have fallen asleep standing up now that all the excitement was over. Alfwyn walked outside and calmed the Rhihalven, telling them to go back to bed. Martina, Heath, and London heeded his advice and headed up the stairs to their room.

Chapter 14 - Breaking Ground

Martina awoke later that morning to blinding light glaring through the window of their tower bedroom. The sunlight reflecting off the snow caused everything to sparkle and glow.

Martina rolled over and closed her eyes tightly. Just a few more minutes was all she wanted. She smiled to herself in her half-sleep. She couldn't help it. The three of them had single-handedly defeated the evil Malandros. Because of them, the Rhihalven were safe. At least for now. Martina opened her eyes.

What was it that Malandros had said? Something about a bigger plan after he destroyed us? What was his bigger plan? And who is their great leader? Her furiously spinning thoughts completely awakened her. What was Malandros trying to accomplish by making the Rhihalven remember the past?

Just then, Heath groaned and sat up in bed stretching. He pulled his knees up as he shoved the covers to the foot of the bed. Running a hand through his curly, disheveled hair, he yawned and rested his elbows on his knees. "What the heck is that light?"

Martina swung her legs over the edge of the bed while London buried her face deeper in her pillow. Heath grabbed his own pillow and threw it across the room at London. She let out a squeal as it hit the wall above her head and fell on top of her.

"It's a good thing you play tuba and not baseball," London called as she turned her face toward the other wall.

A light knock sounded at their door, and it opened before they could reply.

"You three had better get dressed." Parisa hustled into the room with a stack of clean clothes for them. "Alfwyn has been at a meeting for the last hour explaining to everyone in Rhihalvberg what happened last night." Ilona toddled into the room. "He told me briefly this morning what happened. I am excited to hear your explanation. The town is waiting for you."

"We have to explain everything to all the Rhihalven?" London asked, obviously nervous. Her big green eyes showed no sign of sleepiness anymore.

"The Rhihalven will not be angry," Parisa assured them. "They just need to understand exactly what happened. If anything, they will be happy that Malandros is gone."

They quickly showered and got ready to talk to the Rhihalven. After a fast breakfast, they passed through Alfwyn's office, led by Parisa and Ilona, and out onto a large patio set up like an amphitheater at the back of the house.

Alfwyn's voice echoed across the stone seats as he answered questions from the crowd. A hush fell over the group as Martina, Heath, and London approached his podium and stood on both sides of Alfwyn.

Looking out on the crowd, Martina shivered. The entire town must have been there. Hundreds of Rhihalven all had their eyes on them. Martina swallowed and met Alfwyn's gaze.

"Most of you have seen our three human visitors, Martina, Heath, and London," Alfwyn said.

Martina and London gave a slight wave to the crowd. Heath raised both fists triumphantly in the air, and Martina quickly pinched his side so he put them back down.

Alfwyn turned to the trio. "And now, will you please explain to everyone what happened last night?" Alfwyn asked.

Martina nodded and stepped forward. "It all started in the Garden of Alfalonga." She gave the Rhihalven details of everything from finding the Diana's Eye to defeating Malandros. She omitted the line that Heath had suggested would spice up their story and tried to make everything as simple as possible. When she finished, she took a deep breath and looked back at Alfwyn. "Is that all?" she asked.

"I think we have a few questions." Alfwyn gestured to the crowd, which was murmuring wildly.

Martina, Heath, and London took questions for almost half an hour, until one Rhihalva called out, "Who were the others in league with Malandros?" Then someone yelled, "What is the big plan Malandros talked about?"

Alfwyn discussed the Sychateros and how they were supposedly extinct. Most of the Rhihalven didn't know what a Sychatero was, so that took a while to explain. He revealed that those seen in the streets had been thawed and taken to an undisclosed location where they would be secluded from other creatures and under heavy surveillance. Finally, Caelestis, the weather Rhihalva, stood and looked sternly at Heath.

"So where is my snowglobe now, boy?" Caelestis asked.

Heath dug into his pockets and fished it out. Upon handing it back, he grinned at Caelestis. "I guess you will want to make it snow more often now, huh?"

Caelestis's face turned grey. "Absolutely not," he exclaimed. "That snowglobe has not been used in hundreds of years."

"Why do we *not* use the snowglobe, Caelestis?" Alfwyn asked.

"I have never been able to find an explanation for it," Caelestis explained. "I have searched the books on weather dating back for a thousand years and cannot find anything. The tornadoes are obvious enough, but snow is beyond me."

"Then perhaps it would not hurt, if every once in a while, we could have snow here," Alfwyn said. "It is lovely to look at and so delightfully cold. It would be a pleasant change after a few warm days, do you agree?"

Caelestis rubbed his temple. "I cannot think of a reason why not."

The group clapped and cheered with excitement.

"I can teach you all how to make a fort and have snowball fights," Heath called out to the crowd. Puzzled, everyone stared at him. Martina nudged him.

"The Rhihalven probably don't understand fighting for fun, Heath," she whispered through clenched teeth.

"I'll show you how to build a snow Rhihalva," Heath yelled.

The crowd began chattering excitedly.

Just then, another member of the audience stood. As Arist smoothly rose to his feet, all eyes turned to him. He brushed some of his shining hair off his forehead and smiled broadly at the crowd. "I have an idea." He looked around as if to be certain he had the full attention of the audience. "I would like to build something to bring the community closer together after such stressful events."

Alfwyn smiled and nodded to him. He picked up the model of the carousel that he usually kept on his desk and handed it to Arist.

Arist glanced around at the assembled group, which was, by now, dancing in their seats with anticipation. With a flourish of his arms and a gesture toward the model, Arist continued. "Imagine, if you will, an enormous rotating platform with replicas of all sorts of animals fastened to it. There would be an enormous covering to go over this platform, which would keep the sun and the rain from ruining the beautifully painted animals."

The crowd nodded, appearing somewhat unsure.

Arist flashed his brilliantly white teeth and continued. "Not only would the platform rotate, but it would also play music. And the animals would go up and down as if they were really moving on their own." Arist gazed lovingly at the model in his hands.

"That is not the best part, though. Everyone would be able to ride the animals on this rotating platform that plays music." He scanned the crowd, likely looking for approval.

"What do you call this creation?" one Rhihalva asked from the back row.

"I have not thought of a name, yet," Arist explained.

"Call it a 'carousel,'" Heath offered. He gave Martina and London an ornery smile.

"We have them back home. It's a great idea," Martina added. Heath looked at her abashed. Apparently, he wanted to be remembered in Rhihalvberg as the one who named the carousel.

Arist did not look pleased about his spotlight being taken away. He furrowed his brow as if in thought, then held a finger in the air. "Splendid," he said. "Now we have to decide where to put it."

"I could have our cartographer adjust our main street enough to put a park in the middle," Alfwyn said. "That would be convenient for everyone. Would that work?"

"That would be perfect," Arist replied. His lips clicked back into his smiling position a little too suddenly. His eyebrows lowered again so his face took on the look of a lion about to pounce on its prey.

Martina looked quickly at Alfwyn, but he didn't look alarmed. She assumed, then, that Arist always looked like this when he got his way.

Eventually, the meeting came to a close and the trio returned to the house with Alfwyn, Parisa, and their children.

"Let us have a celebratory banquet tonight," Alfwyn announced once they were inside. "Our guests deserve it. And later I will present Siofra with the Diana's Eye, to return to its rightful owner."

"I don't really want to leave," Martina said, "but I think after the banquet tonight would be a good time. We have a long summer ahead of us, and I miss my family." She glanced awkwardly at the floor. "I never thought I'd say that," she thought.

"That is certainly understandable," Parisa said. "You three need to relax. You spent so much time and effort trying to find the Diana's Eye." Parisa hurried off toward the kitchen. "I will tell our cook to have a nice big meal prepared for dinner."

*   *   *   *
*   *

Immediately after dinner, Martina, Heath, and London went back to their tower bedroom. After Martina was packed, she stared out the window. The town looked so strange iced with the snow that they had caused. Some of the Rhihalva children were playing in their yards. Parents stood in doorways and on porches shaking their heads in disbelief. Thousands of childhoods had passed in this town without anyone ever knowing what it was like to build a snow Rhihalva, go sledding, or eat snow. Martina smiled. They looked like they were having fun.

Heath joined her at the window and stood silently for a moment. "We better get going. The sun is starting to set, and before we go, Alfwyn wanted to show us something."

Leaving the backpack in their room, the trio ran down the stairs to the front hall. Their hosts were outside enjoying the snow. Martina, Heath, and London opened the front door and walked outside. The adults stood up and looked at them sadly.

"We have enjoyed having you here. I hope you come visit us again." Parisa gathered them all and hugged them tightly.

"Next time, let us hope you get to enjoy all the wonderful things Sheardland has to offer," Alfwyn said, "instead of spending the whole time on an adventure." He shook his head. "I have a feeling the Sychateros will not be up for any mischief for a while. Most of them are still thawing out from their experience this morning." Alfwyn let out a sly laugh.

"Was there not something we were going to show them, Alfwyn?" Parisa asked.

"Yes, of course. I almost forgot." He smiled. "The trolley should be here any minute. Actually, I have two things to show them."

The gleaming green trolley slowed to a stop in front of Adalborg. Chavdra waved cheerfully at them from the driver's seat. "This snow is gorgeous. I have never seen anything so beautiful. It makes the whole town look like a cake!"

As the trolley spun along the ground for a few blocks, Martina noticed it sprayed a dusting of snow each time it skimmed the road. Soon, the trolley stopped, and everyone followed Chavdra from the vehicle.

Walking toward a tall, wiry woman, Alfwyn held up his palm in greeting. Light bounced between his palm and hers.

She was strikingly beautiful. She smiled broadly, revealing dazzlingly white teeth, but nearly concealing her dark brown eyes. The woman wore a mocha-colored dress and an olive cape edged with shimmery gold embroidery which all contrasted nicely with her shoulder-length, chocolate brown hair.

Then, Alfwyn introduced Martina, Heath, and London to Demetria, the cartographer.

Demetria bowed toward them. "Thank you for your effort in finding the Diana's Eye. You saved us from those awful nightmares."

The trio grinned.

"I know you are curious," Alfwyn said. "So I brought you to the location for the new carousel so you can see how land is created here." Then, he turned back to Demetria and began discussing the size of lot that was needed for the carousel, right there by the road.

Once the plan was set, Demetria waved her hand, conjuring a table with a map on it. The map was a small replica of the one from Alfwyn's office that showed all of Sheardland.

Martina watched as she scanned it for the area where they were standing and magnified the map. Dipping a quill in the onyx black ink that was on the table, she touched the tip to the page. Instantly, the ground in front of them began to tremble. Then, Demetria made a few small adjustments to the page.

The trio stood in shock for a moment.

The nearby earth, which had been covered by two buildings situated side by side, now stretched like soft green chewing gum as they watched. Creaks and groans filled the air as everything shifted to make room for the new lot. When Demetria was satisfied, she set the quill down and waved her arms, causing the table and map to disappear.

The newly created area bubbled and snapped until the ground finally settled with a loud sigh. Demetria turned to the others. "How does it look? Is this the right size for the carousel and park?" she asked.

Alfwyn laid a hand on her arm and smiled broadly. "Perfect."

"That was so awesome!" Heath said.

Soon everyone had piled back into the Lollie Trolley. Chavdra took them around to the Garden of Afalonga and pulled back hard on a lever. The trolley jolted upward, flying them toward the place where, just the night before, they had climbed around the mountain and gazed out on the white emptiness of the undeveloped area.

The triplets, who hadn't had much to say the entire trip, now chattered excitedly about it. It didn't last long, however, because Chavdra landed the Lollie Trolley on the edge of the entrance to the cave. A hush fell over the group.

Alfwyn strode toward the cave, his cape billowing in the light breeze that blew over the snowy access. The group followed cautiously behind him.

"I thought I would never have to come back here again," Martina whispered to her friends.

"The Sychateros are all gone," Heath said, "so there is nothing to worry about."

"Still," Martina said. She just couldn't shake that creepy feeling.

As they entered, their footsteps echoed off the rocky walls. Drawing nearer to the empty pond, Alfwyn stopped and gestured toward a side hall that left the main chamber of the cave. "It is down here," he said.

The group continued to follow him, anxious but not willing to emit a sound. Finally, they entered a room filled with crates and lit by torches on the wall.

"What's in the crates?" Heath asked.

"We were hoping you might know," Alfwyn said. "We have never seen these before, so I wanted you to be here when we opened them." Alfwyn shoved a crate toward them and pried open the lid. "We thought it might be a human production." Inside was a large deflated bag with the remnants of a milky white substance inside. He pulled out the bag to show them. As he did, a cap caught on the side of the crate.

"Maybe if we open that cap, someone will recognize the smell," London suggested.

Alfwyn gingerly turned the cap with his fingers and held onto the opening. He sniffed it. "It smells very sweet," he said. "And the cap is sticky."

"Wait a second. Let me see that," Martina said. She stepped forward and plunged her finger into the opening of the bag.

"No," London said. Her face was wrinkled in disgust.

"Don't you always yell at me for eating strange things?' Heath asked.

Despite their protests, Martina tasted the liquid that was on her finger and smiled at the group. "It's ice cream mix. This must be all the bags that have been stolen from the Sundae Best for the past several months," she said.

"It's always been my dream to drink ice cream mix," Heath said. "Someone was very lucky."

"But what are the crates doing in this cave?" Torvald asked.

"It's all coming together now," Martina nearly shouted. "The Sychateros lived here, and they stole the Diana's Eye. They must have stolen the ice cream while they were on the surface, too. That also explains why the candy was missing from the chemist's shop. The Sychateros eat a lot of sugar. It all fits perfectly!"

"It's bound to be sweeter than anything we have in Sheardland," Alfwyn added. "And Sychateros do keep a high-sugar diet to stay warm in the water."

"Everything makes sense now," London exclaimed.

"Except one thing," Heath reminded them. "What did Mr. Willoughby leave Teagan this for?" Heath pulled his hand out of his pocket and opened it, revealing the watch. He pressed the button on the side, and they were greeted with a beeping that echoed cacophonously off the close walls. "I traded Teagan for this." Heath grinned at Martina and London.

Alfwyn pressed the button again as he took the watch from Heath, and everyone took their hands off their ears, blinking as they recovered from the inundation of noise. "This would have come in very handy for you last night, judging from the performance it just gave." He smiled.

No one said a word as they gazed puzzled at Alfwyn.

"Sychateros do not have the best sight as they like to spend so much time in the water," Alfwyn began, "however, they do have extra-sensitive hearing. If Martina had this watch on last night in the water, she probably would have confused them so much when they started chasing her that you would have escaped a lot easier. The beeping would have clouded their hearing and scrambled their thoughts so much that they would have bumped into each other trying to figure out where it was coming from." He laughed. "Leaving it in the water would have kept them busy for a long time, at least long enough for you to run down the hill and back to the house. Of course, Malandros would not have been stopped then." Alfwyn handed the watch back to Heath who crammed it into his pocket. "I guess it was for the best that you did not use it." He patted Heath's shoulder. "Even Artemidoros Willoughby is not always right."

The group clambered back into the Lollie Trolley. It seemed that all the mysteries had been solved, but Martina wondered about one last thing.

"Why do you think Malandros was so set on revealing the ancient past to the Rhihalven?" Martina asked. That question had been on her mind all day.

"Yeah, what good would that do?" London asked.

"That is something I cannot answer." Alfwyn sighed. "I am sure there is a devious plot being cooked out there somewhere. We will search every corner of Rhihalvberg to find out who was helping with it. Malandros mentioned a leader, so he did not act alone. We will have to put some effort into figuring out who that might be. Perhaps whoever he was working with will not be able to finish the plan without him. That is what I am hoping for." Alfwyn smiled at the children and moved the crate back against the wall, closing the conversation.

Martina looked at Heath and London and shrugged. Maybe Alfwyn was right, she thought. She tried to shake the nagging feeling that this wasn't the last of the difficult fights for the Rhihalven. It worried her that they didn't understand evil the same way she, Heath, and London did. And somehow, Mr. Willoughby had known at least some part of it all. But how?

Finally, the Lollie Trolley landed in front of Adalborg. "Thank you for helping us," Chavdra told Martina, Heath, and London as she shook their hands vigorously, obviously proud of knowing this human custom. "Without you, that crazy Rhihalva would still be running free." With that, she turned and waved goodbye. Then, the Lollie Trolley whirled off down the street.

Parisa was waiting for them. "You should gather your things. It is getting late."

Martina, Heath, and London walked back up the stairs to their room. Heath scooped up his backpack, and London checked under her bed.

As they left the room, Martina took one last look. She watched as the furniture again disappeared, leaving an empty room to echo their retreating footsteps and a growing emptiness inside her. She would miss this place. Her family meant so much to her, and she was looking forward to seeing them again. But for several days, this had been her home. It made her sad to think she wouldn't be able to wake up and look across the room to see her two friends. She wouldn't see the sky streaked with every imaginable color as the sun rose and set. She closed the door, took a deep breath, and headed down the stairs to join the others.

When they reached the bottom, Alfwyn was ready with the Dechronstructive potion. They each drank their vial of violet fluid and hugged the Branimirs. Walking back down the street, Martina looked longingly at the houses and stores they were leaving. Faces peered out at them from the windows. Rhihalven smiled and waved at the humans who had saved them from whatever Malandros was planning.

Feeling a little better, Martina waved back. She was proud of what she had done. Taking hold of the door handle at Rhihalva Travel, she glanced back at the town.

"I hope we can come back to visit soon." Heath rubbed his hands together menacingly. "I have three particular young Rhihalven to corrupt. I think it's time they learned how to play some real games."

The trio walked back through Rhihalva Travel, through the room full of blue bubble-like lights, and into the tunnel. As they started climbing the stairs, they heard the echo of what sounded like singing throughout the tunnel. It was the same singing they had heard when they entered before.

"Oh no," Martina said. "With all the excitement, I forgot to ask if Alfwyn knew where that singing was coming from."

Suddenly, out of nowhere, something small and quick streaked past their feet and headed down the tunnel. Heath cried out for the creature to stop, and it turned, dashing back to where they were. It was yet another Sock Gnome, this one with a long dark beard and spectacles. He nervously wrung his hands and gazed at Heath.

"Do you know where that sound is coming from?" Heath asked the anxious creature.

"I am not supposed to tell," the Sock Gnome said in a high, nasally voice, "but because you know that we are in the tunnels anyway . . ." he glanced quickly around the tunnel, "I suppose I can tell you. When representatives from the noble Sock Gnome Nation are on our way to jobs during the night, we sneak through the barrier and sing merrily on our way to the vents. It helps us to keep from being nervous about our missions."

"And to think we were afraid of that." Heath laughed.

London smiled, and Martina bent to speak with the little Gnome. "We promise to keep your secret," she said.

They waved goodbye to the Sock Gnome as they headed off in separate directions.

Once they reached the top of the stairs, Martina almost didn't want to go back through the ice cream machine. Leaving Sheardland meant that she and Heath would have to face London moving soon. Determined to stay upbeat, she turned to the others. "It's so exciting that we are the only ones who know any of the stuff that has happened down here."

"Just us and the Rhihalven," Heath said.

Martina turned the handle. "Are we ready?" They nodded, and she slowly pushed open the door that led into the ice cream shop.

Chapter 15 - Teagan's Treasure

Nearly a week later, Martina was sitting on the porch enjoying the warm early summer evening. She had just painted her toenails bright pink, and was dangling her feet from the porch swing while she read a Nancy Drew novel. Wind rippled her hair as she swung gently.

She was enjoying spending time with her family and friends and actually found her chores to be a relief when compared to being chased by the Sychateros. Her adventure in Sheardland had been fun overall, but some of it she could have done without. She really had loved helping the Rhihalven, though many times, she found herself feeling uncomfortable. And somehow, she felt older and wiser from the experience. And definitely braver. She started to wonder what more she was capable of, now that she had a taste of adventure.

Lazily, she watched the moving van across the street as people walked in and out for hours. Someone had finally bought the empty house across from hers. She wondered what type of family would be living there, hoping it would be someone interesting. At that moment, she was nearly knocked out of the swing by the force of someone suddenly pushing it.

Grabbing the front of the swing before she fell off, she jerked her head around, expecting to see Teagan.

"What are you doing out of bed?" she cried as she struggled to keep herself and her book from hitting the ground.

Heath grinned and jumped onto the porch. "I'm completely better." He leaned against the support post.

"I'm glad you're better," Martina said. "I'm also glad you didn't come over here with that nasty funk you had all week. Who knows how contagious you were?"

"The monsters in my attic didn't catch it," Heath said, "but Mom probably taught them a curse to repel viruses."

"I see that all that time you spent in bed didn't dampen your spirits any." Martina laughed.

"Actually, I slept on the bathroom floor for several days. Mom says I haven't been that sick in a long time." Heath crossed his arms. "I felt so rotten all week I couldn't move. Most of the time, I slept. But, it seemed like something was constantly bursting out of my body. My eyes were watering, my nose was running, I was throwing up, and—"

"That's enough." Martina cut him off. "Thanks for the play-by-play, but I'd rather you just say you were sick." Martina poked his chest. "So where have you been all day if you've been feeling all right?"

"I see." Heath nodded and kerplunked down on the top step. He put his hand over his heart. "You missed me terribly. You must have felt worse than I did from having to live without me all week." He reached out a hand to pat Martina's.

"Actually, my days have been pretty full," Martina said. "After working at the Sundae Best today, Nancy and I," she held up her book, "have been out here watching the moving van. It's very exciting," Martina said. "So what did you do?"

"This morning I slept in," Heath said, "ate some marshmallow flake cereal thing because I'm on that health food kick. Then I watched some TV."

"Sounds fun," Martina said. "Do you want to come inside? I was thinking about a snack before you came."

The two went in Martina's house and began to make nachos in the kitchen. Martina had just finished convincing Heath that ketchup would be seriously detrimental to the taste when the doorbell rang. Heath peered out the window as Martina popped the bowl into the microwave.

"Know anyone with a blue bike?" Heath asked.

"Not that I can think of," Martina said.

"Hey, guys."

Martina and Heath turned around to see London standing there. Mom had just let her in.

"Did you find out when you're moving?" Martina was afraid to hear her answer.

"Yeah, today," London began. "I've been so busy packing all week that I didn't have time to tell you guys."

"But where did your parents find a house?" Martina replied.

"Look out the window," London said. "It's right across the street."

"Are you serious?" Martina cried.

"That is so great," Heath exclaimed. "Now we can all hang out all the time."

"I don't know," London said. "We never do anything exciting," she teased.

*   *   *   *   *   *

After dinner, Teagan followed Martina up the stairs. "Can you play Scary Ugly Combat Monsters with me?" he asked. He jumped up and down, pulling on the back of her shirt, just before she made it to the safety of her room.

"I guess." Martina braced herself against the doorway. She almost felt like she missed being around Teagan after all the time she had spent away from him. At least he wasn't like the droning agreeable robots that the Branimir boys seemed to be. Trying to shake the feeling of endearment she was beginning to have for her brother, she entered his room to play cards with him.

"Show me how to play," Martina said.

"First, you have to see my new cards," Teagan said. He dug through a bin and pulled out two of the ugliest Scary Ugly Combat Monsters trading cards that Martina had ever seen. Then he dumped the entire bin on the ground and began shuffling the deck by smearing them around.

"When did Mom buy you new cards?" Martina asked. She stifled her urge to snatch up the cards and shuffle them herself.

"She didn't," Teagan said. He stared intently as he mixed the cards. "I traded Heath that broken watch for them."

"Really?" Martina smiled.

"I think I got the better deal," he answered. "One has wings so it can fly over battles. That means it gets more points . . ."

Martina didn't hear the rest.

For about an hour, they played, and then she returned to her own room when their mom told Teagan to get ready for bed. As she checked her email, she glanced out the window at London's new house. She couldn't believe that London would be living so close to her now. It had been wonderful getting to know her better on their adventure. They had been friends before, but now, Martina felt so much closer to her.

When the phone rang, Martina answered. It was Heath.

"I wondered if you wanted to hang out at my pool tomorrow. I'm warning you ahead of time that I'll be over early to wake you up," Heath said. "I'll give London a wake-up call, too. I haven't decided which song from the Tuba Jungle Symphony I'll play. Do you have a favorite animal you want it to be about?"

"How about a three-toed sloth?" Martina paused. "Hey, Heath. I played cards with Teagan tonight, and he showed me those two cards you traded him. That was pretty clever."

"I know," Heath responded. "I can't believe you all thought the watch was broken. I mean, who actually leaves someone a broken watch in their will. Well, unless you wanted to insult someone." He chuckled. "That would be hilarious, actually."

"It would be unusual," Martina said.

"Do you really think Alfwyn will contact us when the carousel is ready?" Heath asked.

"Of course. We really helped them out," Martina said. "By the way, guess what I heard on the news? The flooding in Asia stopped. And the water is going down. I wonder how that happened. Hmm."

"Yeah, I wonder." Heath laughed.

"I better get to bed," Martina said. "See you tomorrow."

"Bright and early," Heath said.

After hanging up, Martina got ready for bed and lay down on top of her maroon comforter. But she couldn't get comfortable on anything since she had slept on the giant woolly worm hair mattress. Her own bed just couldn't compare. She sat up and hugged her fish pillow to her chest. It reminded her of the Diana's Eye.

It was so crazy that Diana's Eye was a major force in controlling the tides and the moon but that only three people knew about it. Gradually, her musings drifted back to Sheardland.

Out of habit, she reached for the key that she had gotten used to wearing around her neck. But it was safe in the secret compartment in her music box. She missed the weight and warmth of the key against her chest.

She reached for the music box and wound the back. She opened the lid and lay down again, trying to get comfortable.

As the gentle melody drifted through the room, mingling with the warm breeze that floated through her bedroom window, Martina closed her eyes. Soon, she dreamed of carousels, snapdragons, and swimming pools. She knew she was bound for more adventures soon, starting with her morning alarm.

ABOUT THE AUTHOR

CORI NICOLE SMITH holds BAs in both English and biology and an MA in English from West Virginia University. Her manuscript for *Martina Mackenzie: The Diana's Eye* was a semi-finalist, ranked in the top 100 submissions, in the Amazon Breakthrough Novel Award Contest in 2008. She edited the novel *Ordinary People Extraordinary Planet* (authored by Dr. Shellie Hipsky), based on interviews from the radio show of the same name.

Since October of 2005, she has worked as a technical writer and editor while writing and polishing her novels. She and her husband and children reside in Washington, Pa., a short distance from Bridgeport, W.Va. where she grew up.

.

CPSIA information can be obtained at www.ICGtesting.com
Printed in the USA
BVOW08s0033200416

444863BV00001B/2/P